Richard Deare Pierpoint

In Uganda for Christ

The Life Story of the Rev. John Samuel Callis B. A., of the Church Missionary Society

Richard Deare Pierpoint

In Uganda for Christ
The Life Story of the Rev. John Samuel Callis B. A., of the Church Missionary Society

ISBN/EAN: 9783337162689

Printed in Europe, USA, Canada, Australia, Japan

Cover: Foto ©Raphael Reischuk / pixelio.de

More available books at **www.hansebooks.com**

IN UGANDA FOR CHRIST

THE LIFE STORY OF THE REV. JOHN SAMUEL CALLIS B.A., OF THE CHURCH MISSIONARY SOCIETY

By the Rev.

R. D. PIERPOINT M.A

RECTOR OF WEST HALTON

With a Preface by the Rev. H. S. Fox, M.A., Honorary Secretary of the C.M.S

WITH PORTRAIT AND
ILLUSTRATIONS

LONDON

HODDER AND STOUGHTON

27 PATERNOSTER ROW

1898

Preface

I HAVE been honoured by the invitation to prefix a few words to the brief story of a young Missionary. I do so with thankfulness and hope, believing that the simple narrative both illustrates a gracious fact and sets forth a wholesome example. In my acquaintance with those who have received the Missionary call, I have been struck by the number who come of a godly seed. The old taunt that the children of pious parents turn out ill, is only based on exceptions which secure prominence by their rarity. On the other hand, as it should be, the instincts created by the Spirit through the influences of a holy home are the commonest causes for Missionary ambition. While there is no such thing as hereditary grace, there is a power in parental prayers, and a holy family history which, without the smallest human suggestion, nay, sometimes in most unlikely ways, prepares the soul for God's leadings into the Missionary life.

v

The unaffected story of John Samuel Callis is not that of a man of exceptional genius or extraordinary attainments. He was a fair type of a thoughtful, quiet young Englishman, sincere and pious, consistently living up to his knowledge of God's will. It is this which gives the book its special value. His example is no unattainable ideal, and for that reason may be the better stimulus for many a man to whom it will say, "Go thou and do likewise." The strength of our Lord's story of the Good Samaritan is that it tells of an act of simple charity within the reach of every one—of the same kind is the present memoir. And thus even the early loss of our dear young brother may, in God's way of loving wisdom, become as the corn seed dying unto life, and bearing much fruit in the Eternal Kingdom of our Lord.

H. E. F.

March, 1898.

Contents

CHAPTER I

PAGE

CHILDHOOD AND EARLY DAYS 1

CHAPTER II

COLLEGE LIFE AND PREPARATION FOR THE MINISTRY . 10

CHAPTER III

THE THREE YEARS' MINISTRY AT ALL SAINTS', PLUM-
STEAD 28

CHAPTER IV

THE MISSIONARY CALL AND DISMISSAL TO THE MISSION
FIELD 41

CHAPTER V

THE VOYAGE TO AFRICA AND STAY IN FRERE TOWN 57

CONTENTS

CHAPTER VI

PAGE

THE JOURNEY TO THE FRONT 78

CHAPTER VII

ARRIVAL IN UGANDA AND DEPARTURE FOR TORO . . 119

CHAPTER VIII

JOURNEY TO TORO 131

CHAPTER IX

AT WORK IN TORO 147

CHAPTER X

THE EARLY HOME CALL 156

Chapter I

CHILDHOOD AND EARLY DAYS

"The Lord called Samuel: . . . Samuel did not yet know the Lord, neither was the word of the Lord yet revealed unto him."—1 *Sam.* iii. 4 7.

JOHN SAMUEL CALLIS was born at 43, Berners Street, Ipswich, on Wednesday, March 30th, 1870. He was the third child and eldest son of John and Sarah Callis. His father had been for five years curate of St. Margaret's in that town. The eldest daughter, Margaret Wells, died at Norwich in 1889; and the second, Ellen Mary, was married in 1895 to the Rev. Edward Symonds, vicar of Walton, near Felixstowe. The first lessons for the day (March 30th) were 1 Samuel i. and ii. (Old Lectionary). This suggested the name of the son of the prayerful Hannah as an appropriate one. This honoured name was also borne by the esteemed vicar, the Rev. Samuel Garratt by whom the infant was baptized on April 30th, when he received the Christian names of John Samuel. A note in the father's diary reads: "The dear little man behaved very well. May he lead the rest of his life according to this beginning." One of the god-parents was the Rev. R. D. Pierpoint, at that time curate of St. Clement and St. Helen's, Ipswich, now rector of West Halton, Lincolnshire, the compiler of this memoir.

The little Samuel's early life was marked by some delicacy of constitution, but in after years he developed into a strong and healthy man. It was hoped that the climate of that part of the mission field to which he was subsequently directed might prove to be of the very best for him. This was Bishop Tucker's expectation. In a letter written to his father at that time, he says: "I may say that Toro is a wonderfully healthy country, and I shall be greatly surprised to hear of sickness among the missionary party there." But God's "thoughts are not as our thoughts, nor His ways as our ways."

He had from his very earliest years a very tender conscience, and would never go to sleep without seeking his nurse's (Deborah Farthing) forgiveness for any disobedience during the day. When quite a young child he seems to have got into his mind the idea of being a missionary. On one occasion he drew his nurse's attention to a number of cats in the garden grouped together as if they were holding a meeting, and remarked, " I will be good and brave, because I want to be a man and go to the heathen ; I should have to give them meetings." And so it came about, in sober, serious earnest, in the providence of God.

In the spring of 1873 Mr. Callis, having been elected by the trustees of St. George's Vicarage, Battersea, to succeed the Rev. Burman Cassin, the family removed to London. Here the children, then five in number, enjoyed good health taking almost daily exercise in the spacious and beautiful park near by.

After a sojourn at St. George's of little more than two years, on the invitation of the late Bishop of Norwich, the Hon. and Right Rev. John Thomas Pelham, the family again removed, in 1875, to Holy Trinity (South) Heigham Rectory, Norwich, a large suburban parish. Here, first under the kindly instruction of his excellent governess, Miss Searle, and afterwards at a preparatory school for boys, John passed through the usual elementary course of study before entering the grammar school.

Miss Searle says of him : "He was a delicate child, of a sensitive, highly nervous temperament. He had a great dread of strangers, and it was always very difficult to get him to go into the drawing-room when any visitors were there. He was singularly humble-minded, even when quite young, and always noticed anything in others which seemed indicative of pride. It was a long time before he could be induced to use a capital *I* when writing of himself, and he would say when corrected, ' It seems so *proud* to put a capital *I* for yourself. No ; I don't wish to do it, it is so *proud*.' He was generally obedient, and gave little trouble, but could be very determined when he had made up his mind.   I believe God's Holy Spirit was working in him from his earliest infancy. He was always very sorry when he had been naughty, and, although sometimes unwilling to confess at first, I never knew him tell an untruth.   He was quiet, thoughtful, painstaking, and very fond of Bible reading.   He always loved to read and talk about the call of Samuel, and often said, ' When God calls me, I will be like Samuel : I will get up and go directly.   But how shall I know that it is God calling me ?   How shall I be able to tell that it is God's voice ? '   When the great call *did* come, there was no mistaking it ; and, undoubtedly, he did what he promised : he arose and went directly. He was always especially interested in God's plan of redemption, in our Saviour's life, death, and rising again. Although very timid in some things, he was always brave and quiet when any real danger was near. Once, when at Cromer, he was caught on a sandbank by the tide ; but he showed no alarm, saying quietly, ' Oh, we must ask God to save us,' which we did, and then dashed through the water and reached the shore safely." In a letter written to Miss Searle, just before leaving England, he says : " Thank you for all your help and guidance in past years. I probably owe something to your prayers. Your prayers and those of many Christian friends at this time are very precious. "

But, whilst generally of a grave and thoughtful disposition, he evinced the ordinary fondness for fun and mischief of most boys of his age, even yielding on some few occasions to the temptation to play the truant. From a few words found in his handwriting at this period, he was, however, sensitive to the reproofs of conscience, expressing sorrow that he had not only given pain to his earthly parents, but had grieved his heavenly Father.

In 1881, John entered as a pupil at the Norwich Grammar School, then under the mastership of the Rev. O. W. Tancock.

Mr. Tancock says of him : " The sum of my recollection is that he was one of those quiet, rather silent boys, of considerable strength of character, who make their mark after school is done with, rather than during their schoolboy days. He held his own well in his Form, winning, I believe, a prize now and then. But though he was regular, hard-working, and of good report, he was not notable among his fellows. . . . In work and in games there was a steady, serious way of looking at things, and of doing the work of the day or of the term. But there was nothing to mark him as one who cared to lead others, or to strike out a very decided line for himself. He passed into the Headmaster's Form in due time, and did himself credit, but was without enthusiasm for books. . . There was something wanted, as I thought, to awake the character that was in Callis. That awakening of the real man did not come during school life, I feel sure, and it was to come later, when a wider experience of life, and some needful searchings of heart had disturbed the self in him and done some work in him. Others, no doubt, can tell how the steady, somewhat silent seriousness of character of the boy was directed, ripened, and consecrated into the really earnest, unselfish, and solemn devotion of self and life to the service of the Lord Jesus Christ and the Church in the mission field. The Lord can take, and test, and train, and find useful all natural characteristics so that they work the Father's work to which He sends them."

Mr. Ernest E. (now Judge) Wild, an old schoolfellow, writes : " For many years I had the privilege of intimately knowing J. S. Callis. At Norwich School we were great friends, and that friendship continued at Cambridge, although we were then at different colleges, and, consequently, saw less of each other. Were I asked to describe Callis in a sentence, I should say that he was honourable, vigorous, assiduous. At the school he took an active part in athletics, more particularly excelling at football. ' Rugby ' was then the game and he was hard-working as a ' forward,' and sometimes brilliant. He occasionally addressed the Debating Society, and his speeches were always to the point. I remember, too, his acting on Speech Days. As a classic, he was sound ; he did well at divinity and history. All things he did with his might, thereby setting an example, to us all. Boys do not at the time realize directly

I think, the influence that is exerted over them, for good or ill, by the few among their number who possess strong individualities. But after the lapse of years, when school days are memories, when trivialities are forgotten, one can take a mental review of what has passed, and approximate to a sound judgment of the characters of those with whom one worked and played. Then the athletic demigod and the ascetic bookworm are each known to have been insufficient; while the boy who played his best and worked his best, and both unselfishly, receives his tardy meed of praise. Such an one we learn to reverence. From such an one we anticipate a useful life and cosmopolitan sympathies, in whatever sphere he may move. Such an one was Callis. I deem it an honour to be allowed to write these few unworthy lines in tribute to a noble memory."

John was not successful as a prize-winner, not brilliant, as one of the masters remarked, but a steady worker. On one occasion, however, he carried off the Bishop Pelham's prize for divinity, his papers being, by the testimony of the examiner, very well done. This prize he afterwards found most useful, and greatly valued it. It was a finely bound copy of Bishop Wordsworth's

Greek Testament. It was during his schoolboy days that he was confirmed, choosing to be prepared, with his schoolfellows, by the headmaster. Not being of a demonstrative disposition, there was probably a deeper undercurrent of thought as to the responsibility he was taking upon himself than appeared upon the surface. The Confirmation took place in the Cathedral nave, the choir being under repair. The searching, impressive, and fatherly addresses of Bishop Pelham, always so greatly valued throughout his diocese on these occasions of such solemn moment to the candidates, were listened to with marked attention. But the time for manifesting more openly the dedication of the whole being to the Lord had not arrived with him.

Chapter II

" The Lord came . . . and called as at other times. . . .
Then Samuel answered, Speak ; for Thy servant heareth."
—1 *Sam.* iii. 10.

IN 1888, John left school with the Parker Exhi-
bition for one proceeding to the University.
He entered St. Catharine's College, Cambridge,
in October, as " Master's Sizar," through the kindness of the Rev. Canon Robinson, the Master of
the College. The first year is usually one in
which the character of the student is put to the
severest test. The comparative independence, the
congenial surroundings, the buoyancy of spirit
of early manhood, tend to induce, even those most
carefully trained at home, to yield to the attrac-
tion of the world and its pleasures in the pursuit
of happiness and satisfaction. Though never
yielding to its grosser forms of temptation, the

young freshman was somewhat drawn into the society of those who loved the world and the things of the world. When settling down to the work of preparation for his future life's calling, he for a time passed through greatly troubled waters.

Writing of the life at Cambridge, he says : " There is up here such a strange jumble of Low Church, Broad Church, and those of more 'advanced' ideas—the last decidedly predominating—that, together with innumerable heresies and forms of unbelief, they tend to convert what is *primâ facie* a simple and straightforward religion into a most difficult and intricate science." Possessed of an honest mind, he could find no rest of soul in anything short of truth and reality. For a short time sceptical books seemed to attract him. At another time he seemed to think the truth was on the side of Rome and those who have adopted more or less of her sacerdotal and sacramental theories and practices, whilst remaining professedly members of the Church of England. At one time the life and writings of the late Cardinal Newman and the self-sacrificing labours of Father Damien amongst the lepers, seemed to draw him powerfully towards their communion. Here he seemed to think were models for his own life and work. In

his search for the solid rock of truth, he looked
this way and that for guidance, rather, perhaps,
to the works of religious men than to the pure
word of God.

He was much exercised at this time on the
mysterious subject of the origin of evil—the
dealings of God with the finally impenitent—the
intermediate state—the latter especially in con-
nection with the antagonistic views of the late
Dean Goulburn and of Dean Farrar. He seemed
to incline to the idea that these should be treated
as mere matters of opinion, and not of faith. Scien-
tific objections to facts stated in Scripture seem also
to have troubled him. Writing of the parties in
the Church, he expresses a hope to be able to steer
clear, at any rate for the time, of the teaching of any
party whatever. In 1890 he heard an address of
Rev. J. E. C. Welldon, master of Harrow, a rela-
tive of his mother's. He says: " The stillness was
quite impressive all the time, and it was just the
manly, straightforward sort of address calculated
to tell up here."

The Rev. S. Symonds, of St. Mark's, Newnham,
who was then at Ridley Hall, gives an insight
into John's first years at Cambridge. He writes:
" It was my privilege to see dear Jack very often,
it was at the commencement of his second year,

and I can well remember the circumstances that
had impressed upon him just before the tremendous debt we owe to God. Accordingly, I found
him seemingly seeking for light and rest, and,
for the year that I was with him, he was wander-
ing round in his search for satisfaction. His mind
was too independent to take everything he was
told without inquiring, and consequently he was at
one time much impressed by Kingsley's writings,
at another by Pusey's, I think. He used to say
that, had the representative High Churchmen of
the College been men of backbone, he would probably have thrown in his lot with them. He was
one who fought his way to truth *alone*, I should
say. . . . He was essentially practical, and
mission work which he undertook in Barnwell did
a great deal for him. On one occasion he had a
C.P.A. meeting in his rooms, addressed by the
Rev. J. G. Dixon, of Christ Church, and a meeting
was also got up for Douglas Hooper in J. J.
Woolsey's rooms, which possibly had its effect
upon Jack. I remember going with him to some
open-air mission work in St. Matthew's, Barnwell
where his vigour in holding forth much impressed
me."

The great turning point of his life, through the
gracious influence of the Holy Spirit, appears to

have been on the occasion of the illness and death of his eldest sister, in the year 1889, to whom, as to the others, he was devotedly attached. " I did not know," he writes, on hearing of the opinions of her medical adviser, "that she had been worse lately, and was terribly surprised to hear of her dangerous condition ; notwithstanding the doctors, I still trust health will return with the advent of warm spring weather. It must be a very anxious time for you and mother, and I have thought very much about you. Surely God will not take away one who is so good, so useful, and so dear to us. A friend of mine has this term undergone a bitter bereavement, but, being a true Christian, he could say, in prayer, ' *Thy will be done.*' Would that I could say so now!" In May he was summoned from Cambridge to witness a beautiful example, indeed, of cheerful resignation to the will of God, and to mark that heavenly halo which gathers round a youthful Christian's dying bed. Her " perfect peace " and calm joyousness at the prospect of departing to be "with Christ " greatly impressed him. He was at College when the end came, June 4th ; but returned home to follow the dear mortal remains to their last resting place in the Norwich cemetery. Writing in truest Christian sympathy, a dear friend, then rector of Lowestoft, Canon Nash, suggested that the death of the sister might be the means of life to the brother; and so it seemed to be by the grace of God. From that time there was a decided change in the dear brother, a deeper thoughtfulness concerning spiritual and eternal things, and a more real and earnest seeking after God. The favourite hymn of the beloved sister well expressed the attitude of his own soul afterwards. It is found in the collection of mission hymns used by the late Rev. John Hall Shaw, whose ministry during a mission in her father's parish in 1884 was greatly blessed to her and very many.

"From glory unto glory! our faith hath seen the King,
We own His matchless beauty, as adoringly we sing;
But He hath more to show us! O thought of untold bliss!
And we press on exultingly in certain hope of this.

　　　*　　　*　　　*　　　*　　　*

In full and glad surrender we give ourselves to Thee,
Thine utterly, and only, and evermore to be!
O Son of God, who lovest us, we will be Thine alone,
All we are, and all we have, shall henceforth be Thine own!"

From this time whole-hearted consecration to Christ, and the sacrifice of self in His service, became grand life-principles with him. On a scrap of paper found in one of his commentaries, he wrote: "God wants our best—our bodies, not our purses. Use me, just as, when, where Thou wilt."

During the vacations, especially his earlier ones, he frequently visited his uncles in the midland counties, and, at one time, became very fond of hunting. Some of the pictures in his room spoke of the sporting tastes of those days. His fearless determination was evinced on one of his holiday excursions, in accepting a challenge to mount and ride a high-spirited mare. The animal bolted and threw him, he was carried into the house insensible, and narrowly escaped death.

During the last long vacation in 1890, he spent some weeks at the Charterhouse Mission House in Tabard Street, Southwark. The Rev. P. N. Waggett, leader of the mission at that time, found him a devoted companion and loyal fellow-worker. John writes : " The calm reverence and reality of the congregation drawn from the lowest of Southwark slums was delightful."

He was admitted to the degree of B.A., June 20, 1891, passing satisfactorily in the Theological Special Examination. In a testimonial letter, his College tutor wrote : " As his time of residence advanced, Mr. Callis, too, seemed to advance in seriousness and earnestness of disposition. He would, I believe, perform any duties which he undertook with a conscientious determination to acquit himself to the best of his powers."

In the following August his father took John and his eldest sister, with a cousin, for a tour on the Continent. The beauty and grandeur of the scenery with its mountains and lakes were greatly enjoyed by the whole party, and very notably by him who was destined to look upon some of the most magnificent natural scenery of the world in Eastern and Central Africa.

On this brief tour many cathedrals and churches were visited, and opportunities were thus afforded of observing the system of the Church of Rome in its full development, and in some of her grandest places of worship. It was hoped that this might have a useful effect upon the young candidate for Holy Orders, and so it proved. At first he appeared to be much awed on entering these temples so full of pictures, images, crucifixes, and altars, with all their imposing furniture and apparatus of sacrificial service. But, after a time, he became fully impressed with its unspiritual, sensuous, and materialistic character. Everywhere the highly decorated dolls, representing the Virgin Mother of the Lord, were the most attractive objects of the worshipper's adoration. The Lord of life was every-where still an infant in His mother's arms, or upon the Cross in agony, or, as in Strasburg Cathedral, represented as a lifeless corpse lying across the

2

knees of His distressed mother. Most thankfully, therefore, was the remark received by the father, when it fell from the son's lips, "These people appear to worship a *dead* Christ." Henceforth he seemed to have his thoughts most frequently raised to Him "who *was* dead, but is *alive* for evermore," and "ever liveth" at God's right hand on the eternal throne. It was to a *living*, exalted, reigning Lord and Saviour he delighted to the last to direct the minds and hearts of all amongst whom he ministered, at home and in the mission field.

As John was still by a year and a half too young for ordination, the Rev. Prebendary Webb-Peploe, vicar of St. Paul's, Onslow Square, South Kensington, kindly consented to receive him for a year as one of his lay-workers preparing for Holy Orders. The period was one of great spiritual advantage to him. The faithful and instructive ministry of Mr. Webb-Peploe, the companionship of so many like-minded with himself—all united in the many Christian and philanthropic agencies having St. Paul's, Onslow Square, for their centre—developed in him, by the grace of God, those great Christian principles which are implanted by the Holy Spirit in the soul of every true and devoted servant of Christ. In letters written to his father while at

Chelsea, he says: "I hope you will remember me in prayer that I may be kept in touch with the Source of power and humility." "I had a long talk with a man at the lodging-house, who is apparently utterly blind to spiritual light, and has never, he affirms, had any desire to live a different life. It is so hard to know how to tackle such men, and I feel so young and inexperienced to attempt it." "I had to take our Mission Hall address unexpectedly, quite unprepared, tea-less and tired. The place was quite full, as a special address had been advertised on the Holy Communion. I enjoyed a marvellous sense of the presence of power in answer to prayer." In the visitation of the district assigned to him, and very especially in work in the lodging-houses, where he met with many who had started in life with the fairest prospects, but had made shipwreck of character and all they possessed, he sought with intense earnestness to lead the wanderers and prodigals back to the Father from whom they had gone so far and so long astray. There he manifested much of the loving spirit of the Master who came to seek and to save that which was lost.

The Rev. Prebendary Webb-Peploe writes: "He was a worthy and valuable servant to the

great cause, chiefly marked by the determination
and zeal which carried him forward bravely
through difficulties and temptations." And, again,
in a letter of sympathy written to his father after
his death : "How blessed to know that his life
on earth was one true, faithful, consistent surrender to his Lord's work of all the powers and
wishes that he had ! No ! I may grieve with you
and your family, and the one he hoped to call
'wife,' but I may not forget the blessed reward
of such a good career as your boy's. We thank
God for him, and for his brave career, and rejoice
with you that you have such a son in heaven.
We valued him highly at St. Paul's, and always
look back upon his life among us as one of the
most steadfast and useful of *any* of my young
men ! I have prayed for him daily by name
ever since he came to me, and I shall feel
deeply the pain of leaving his name out of my
list. Three of them—Robinson, Mathias, and
now your boy—have gone home from the mission field, and we can only bow and say, 'Thy
will be done.'"

The Rev. C. E. Barton, missionary in the Punjab,
writes to his father thus : "I always thought of
your son as of others like Robert Stewart of
China, Bishop Hill, Graham Brooke, and Robinson

of West Africa—the key-note of whose lives seemed to be 'To me to live is Christ'—men who lived in the presence of God, and whom He has now called for higher and grander service in the courts above. . . . As you are aware, our acquaintance was but a short one. For about six months or so we worked together as lay-workers under Mr. Webb-Peploe—a great teacher—and, afterwards, I met him once at Woolwich, when he was curate there. What impressed me always was his great strength of purpose. Nothing ever seemed to daunt him ; he went straight ahead, and no difficulties to him seemed insuperable. What I remember best is our work together in a lodging-house kitchen in Chelsea. He and I and my great friend Frank Eardley used to go and visit the unhappy inmates of this den on Sunday afternoons. It was your son who originated the idea. We held a short service, and I can re-member the way he used to stand with his back to a wall, and speak to those men as straight as any one could speak. One poor fellow was rescued from a life of drunkenness and sin, and your son got him taken in by the Church Army Labour Home, where I believe he did very well afterwards. Another man, a prize-fighter, was one your son took a great interest in. The man was an awful drunkard, but he signed the pledge, and kept it, too, for about two months, but then the drink fiend got the better of him, and he broke out again. We were all very disappointed about it, but none more so than Jack Callis. . . Your son was a diligent reader, and in no sense narrow-minded. His deep love for Christ made him love any one who loved Him. He would have made a splendid missionary, as he had the true apostolic spirit."

The Rev. Cecil H. Clissold, one of his fellow-workers at South Kensington, writes : "Jack Callis joined the little group of lay-workers in the poor districts of Prebendary Webb-Peploe's neighbourhood. Our duties were not exactly arduous—the mornings being generally given up to reading, the afternoons to visiting—and the evenings to services in the open air and the mission room. The special department that Jack used to lean to was amongst the men. I well remember on Sunday afternoons after Sunday School, some four or five of us would visit a large men's lodging-house, and hold a service in the great kitchen. It was intensely hot from the great coke fires, and being underground hardly ventilated at all. We used to remove our coats and hats, and take the service in our shirt sleeves.

The singing was led by a cornet, and Jack was usually the speaker. I can see him now with the rough faces around him, reddened in the fire-light, as they listened, almost against their will, to his earnest, forcible words. Now he stretches out his hand to wipe his face, literally steaming with perspiration, owing to the thick close atmosphere, and again he would urge, 'Now, you men, you know you are wrong.' He would appeal to what little remained of their moral feeling and work up from that. Many a quiet talk followed, as he button-holed those whom he detected listening carefully. The regular cadger and hypocrite were not absent. He usually saw through them, but kindness often overruled his better judgment, as he would frequently say afterwards, 'Poor beggar, I feel sure he was lying to me, but it is hard to say No.' This sort of work in Chelsea among the very lowest seemed most congenial to him, and it is worthy of note that, whilst he spoke straight and hit hard, I never remember a serious row ; for, pleading so lovingly with them, they could not quarrel with him.

" I do not know, but I rather fancy that it was whilst here in Chelsea, he caught his missionary ardour, for well I remember our expeditions to Exeter Hall to some great dismissal meetings. But it was amongst the men at the lodging-houses and at the men's services on Sunday evening at the Caroline Place Drill Hall that he did his work when with Prebendary Webb-Peploe. I recollect that his fellow-workers admired him and loved him, although I fancy we did not know half the good he did. He was always so quiet."

The vacations which brought the brother to the home at Norwich from time to time were looked forward to with very much delight by all there, especially the sisters. Great was the joy and excitement when "Johnny" came home from College or his work in London. Many a romp made the walls ring with merry peals of laughter. Pleasant excursions were made upon the river, into the city, the country, and to the seaside. A favourite method of spending a holiday by many in Norfolk is to hire a house-boat and sail and row along the rivers and round the broads of the eastern side of the county. This was also a great delight to John, who sometimes found genial companions for such water trips in his old school-fellows. The experience thus gained, as in the case of Archdeacon Walker of Uganda, no doubt proved of some service to him in after years. Long and deeply interesting conversations were enjoyed

by father and son after the others had retired
to rest; many questions naturally perplexing to
a young and inquiring mind were discussed, it
was hoped with advantage to both. The tendency
to unsettlement in principles and views which
every thoughtful man is sure to experience in
the period of student life sometimes caused his
parents considerable anxiety; but their refuge
was that which never fails—prayer to Him Whose
it is to open the understanding, and to reveal
Christ to the soul in all His sufficiency as the
Christian's "wisdom, righteousness, sanctification,
and redemption." Abundant cause was there, in
the latter days of his life, to praise God that the
years of waiting before Him for His blessing
upon their son John Samuel had not been in
vain. He was indeed deeply taught of God.

For the half-year previous to ordination it
seemed desirable that there should be some re-
tirement from active parish work, and more time
given to reading and prayerful preparation for
the ministry. It was thought that a change of
University for this purpose might be beneficial.
Mr. Webb-Peploe agreed that it would be a
good thing for him to see Oxford life and men
rather than to go back to Cambridge. The Higher
Criticism and Ritual questions were in his opinion

given greater prominence in Oxford thought.
In a letter to his father John thanks him *very*
much for giving him the opportunity of going
to Oxford. A correspondence was opened with
the highly esteemed principal of Wycliffe Hall,
Oxford, the Rev. F. J. Chavasse, and John proceeded to the rooms allotted him there, October
14th, 1892. His first impressions shall be given
in his own words : " Mr. Chavasse is very delightful and sympathetic. After supper in his Lodge
last night, he gave a talk in the Chapel on
' Times of preparation for appointed work,' and
took those of our Lord, St. John the Baptist, and
St. Paul, as typifying their use for learning,
submission, self-denial, and self-consecration. This
morning he had us all individually for arranging
work, etc., in his study. The Chapel is a temporary one, and the services are bright and musical.
. . . Mr. Chavasse's lectures on sermons and
the ministerial life are most helpful." The result
was most satisfactory. The tact and judgment of
the head of that Theological College, with the
kindly and sympathetic nature which have made
him so beloved by his pupils, were a most valuable
means of preparing the young candidate for the
sacred office. The hours of devotion and instruction in the chapel were particularly valued

by him; and the Christian fellowship which the family of students at Wycliffe afforded was also much enjoyed and very helpful. The opportunity of seeing things from an Oxford point of view —with its variety of opinions and religious developments—helped to broaden his mind and sympathies.

During his time there the American evangelist Moody visited the city, and the force of the truth of the gospel, preached, as so often, with the plain, straightforward yet powerful utterances of that devoted servant of Christ, made an impression upon his hearers which greatly astonished many who were somewhat offended at the intrusion into that community of intellect and learning of a teacher who was " mighty" only " in the Scriptures."

The time at Wycliffe passed rapidly and happily away, and it left many reminiscences of true friendships formed and enjoyed, and of spiritual privileges highly valued and greatly profited by. Mr. Chavasse in a letter of sympathy written to his father after his death, writes of that period: " We shall miss him greatly at Wycliffe. He left a bright and fragrant memory behind him. His character had been mellowed and strengthened by conflict and difficulty, and we all felt its influence."

Chapter III

THE THREE YEARS' MINISTRY AT ALL SAINTS' PLUMSTEAD

"We preach not ourselves, but Christ Jesus the Lord; and ourselves your servants for Jesus' sake."—2 *Cor.* iv. 5.
"Instant in season, out of season."—2 *Tim.* iv. 2.

AT the Islington Clerical Meeting, in January, 1893, the Hon. and Rev. Talbot Rice, then vicar of All Saints', Woolwich, was introduced to Mr. Callis, senr., as one seeking a curate. This led, after some communications between them, to the offer and acceptance of his son as a candidate for the vacancy. The parish being in the diocese of Rochester, the ordination took place in the cathedral of that city on Trinity Sunday, May 28th. The Bishop at that time was Dr. Randall Davidson. The next day the newly ordained curate proceeded to the scene of his labours for the next three years. He soon found how wisely all had been ordered for him. For his vicar, to whom he was ever loyal, he had the highest esteem and affection. A new Mission Hall had just been erected in the parish, and here it was part of the

SAINTS' CHURCH, PLUMSTEAD, WOOLWICH

curate's duty to hold a service on Sunday evening. Many were the clubs, unions, associations, and other organizations carried on, with the Mission Hall as a centre, for the benefit of the working population around. Into all these, with the services of the Church and open-air preaching on Woolwich Common and in the streets, John plunged with all the intense earnestness of his character. Almost all the people in his district were Arsenal workers. But amongst the members of the congregation were such men as Rev. Andrew Jukes and Sir S. A. Blackwood. He remarks: " It is rather an ordeal to preach before such deep students of Scripture ; but, as Mr. Chavasse so often reminded us, it is not our message, nor our power, nor are we our own." From notes left, which show the kind of texts usually chosen, it is evident that winning souls to Christ was his one aim and desire. The children of the schools and parish were devoted to him. He knew large numbers by name, and ever greeted them in the street with kindly smile and an affectionate word. His pastoral visitation was a real delight to him.

In November, 1893, the Rev. J. W. Morris succeeded Mr. Talbot Rice as vicar of All Saints'. John gives a graphic account of his welcome, and expresses great thankfulness that he had come.

The following Sunday he expected to have to preach in the morning, address the children in the afternoon, and take the Mission Service at night. " Not so bad," he says, " for a youngster, and no wonder I feel rather like a clock run down." One Sunday he gave a missionary address at the Children's Service in the Garrison Church. He says : " It was rather trying, but it proved a happy time."

John was ordained to the Priesthood at St. James's, Kidbrook, on Trinity Sunday, May 20th, 1894, by the Bishop of Rochester, Dr. Randall Davidson. The preacher on the occasion was the Rev. Canon Streatfield, vicar of Emmanuel Church, Streatham, who took as his text St. John i. 6, 7 : " There was a man sent from God whose name was John," etc. His earnest exhortations to the candidates for the sacred office to take John the Baptist as their model in devotedness to Christ, in humility and courage in bearing " witness to the Light," were well calculated to make a deep and lasting impression upon his hearers.

It will be interesting here to give some details of the young curate's work in All Saints', Plumstead, gathered from letters written by his vicars and other parishioners.

Mr. Talbot Rice writes : " He threw his whole
energy from the first into the work, and visited
most diligently among the poor, finding out some
in out-of-the-way corners whom we had never
discovered. He worked hard with *all* the efforts
that were being made for the good of the parish,
but was specially devoted to the working men,
for whom he very soon started a Club which
went by the name of ' The Magnet,' and was
held in the small room which formed part of a
new Mission Hall of which he was in charge.
. . . He struck me as intensely in earnest and
real, whether in work or in prayer, and in all
personal intercourse with him. I had several most
interesting testimonials, after I left, from residents
in Plumstead, of the influence he had, and of the
way he impressed them. He was most unselfish,
thoughtless almost about himself, if only he might
do more good. . . . One of my regrets at
leaving the parish was leaving him. We only
had three months' actual work together, but one
felt one had in him a real man of God, whose
whole soul was set on winning sinners to Christ
and doing well his Master's work—to work with
whom was a real privilege. He once told me
what had made him deeply enthusiastic for the
gospel of Christ. Standing very late one night

in London outside a public-house, watching the men, and seeing the awful effect of sin on them, he felt it was possible to hope somehow something might save them. He must find the power that could and would, and *that* he felt was in the gospel of God's grace and love in Christ Jesus. One feature of his character was a wholesome contempt for public opinion unless backed by sound principle. On one occasion he deliberately walked round the 'quad' of his own college with one who was very unpopular then, on purpose to help him."

Mr. Morris's testimony is to the same effect. He writes: "His devotion to work and absorption in it was quite remarkable in one so young." In regard to his ministry among working men : "It was his wont not only to visit them regularly, but to follow up weak cases with the most untiring perseverance. He would see men late at night, and would stay with them by the hour, persuading them to see that anything short of a Christian life must be in the long run a life of failure. In temperance work he was a power. He worked, however, on his own lines ; he scarcely ever made a temperance speech, or magnified the importance of the pledge ; but he showed the victims of intemperance that no spiritual progress could be expected unless the obstacle of drink was put away. Often he would go into the public-houses at night, and take men away with him to their homes, reasoning with and comforting them. Seeing, moreover, that pleasures of an innocent nature should be provided as an anti-dote to the 'public,' he begged to be allowed to start a parochial Men's Club. At first no place could be found, but a small room at the back of our Mission Hall was finally fixed upon, and this has ever since been devoted to the men. I hope soon to procure larger and more suitable premises, for many reasons, but, first of all, to perpetuate our gratitude to the founder of this parochial work. . . . A serious outbreak of typhoid fever in 1895 was the means, under God, as far as one can see, of causing Callis to make his mark in the parish. His visiting then was splendid, his patience beautiful. Many a hard heart was at this time softened, and not a few backsliders regained. All parishes have their peculiar difficulties, and one of ours has been the popularity of being called undenominational by many of our earnest people. This Callis set his face against resolutely, as he strongly believed the Church of England provided the fullest and best teaching. I sometimes used to fear that his strong

3

teaching on this matter might upset some of our
poor folk, and defeat the object he had in view ;
but, generally, my fears were groundless. . . .
He was, however, emphatically an *evangelist*.
His preaching was not at all eloquent, but his
intense earnestness seldom failed to impress.
Though so ready to try and cheer others, he was
frequently subject to moods of depression, because
the burden of souls was by him so keenly felt.
It was very difficult to 'get him away from his
work ; and to social life here, in the ordinary sense,
he was a stranger.   He seemed to be always
feeling that there was never time enough to reach
the people, and so was tremendously active even
to the sacrifice of health. Prayer to him was
a glorious reality, and his words, to my mind,
were never so forcible or expressive of his true
character as those uttered on his knees. Open-
air services largely occupied his attention during
the summer and autumn months. His open-air
preaching was much blessed, but, perhaps, chiefly
in stirring up others to come forward in this
direction. One young fellow in another parish,
now in Orders, was singularly helped by the
courage and straightness of Callis's open-air
preaching."

Elizabeth Farrow, the Bible-woman, alluded to

by one of the former vicars as the "one bright spot," in the parish, writes how impressed she was from the time of his first coming to All Saints' with his spirituality of mind, his love of prayer and felt need of it. Whenever a case in the parish had been talked over between them, the end would almost always be, " Let us have some prayer about it—shall we ? " She speaks most warmly of his ministrations during the typhoid epidemic, and how, when he left for a few days to go home during the time, he not only wrote, inquiring after many particular cases by name, but added, " I came away on purpose to have more time with God in prayer for them."

His landlady, Mrs. Clarke, bears significant testimony to his remarkable self-sacrifice and self-denial. Often and often he would give what was prepared for his own meals to the sick, and take it himself to them at all hours of the night, and to those sitting up with the sick likewise. In fact, she says that he was more with his people than in his own rooms, always patiently caring for their troubles, however little, and doing what he could to help them.

The schoolmistress, Miss Cree, writes of his exceeding love for children. It was always his great delight to be with them, and to observe

them both at their work and play. The affection
was, as it generally is, mutual. The last visit
to the schools will never be forgotten. The
girls were repeating Psalm cxxi., and he wrote
afterwards : "How delightful it was to take it
as a last remembrance of the children!" He
asked the children for their prayers. This request was not thrown away. Some days after, a
little fellow about six years of age, when repeating
his ordinary evening prayer, involuntarily added,
"and please keep Mr. Callis's ship off the rocks."
Before the sad news of his death arrived, they
had readily brought their pence (in response to
an appeal from him), to buy Scripture pictures
for the children in Toro. She concludes : "I can
only add from the teachers that we thank God
He allowed us to know him."

A fellow-worker with our dear brother during
the typhoid epidemic (Mrs. Griffiths) writes :
"Never shall I forget that dear Mr. Callis. He
worked so hard with his much-loved people that
once I was really afraid for him because he saw
no danger. One case was that of a poor woman
and her two little children, who were smitten
down. When I arrived, he was trying to wash
the poor dear children, although (as he said) he
did not know how. This was just like him. He

would see into anything that he thought would help the poor people, and thus won many to the Mission Hall. His love for them was a real love, deep and true, pointing them to the Saviour. In that same room, when that mother and children had been removed to the hospital, he began to work again, taking down the bed where the fever-smitten ones had lain, and carrying it downstairs. Then he began to clean the room. On another occasion there was a man nearly out of his mind. Mr. Callis stayed with him alone, and never left his bed until some one came and took his place. He was never weary in well-doing. He was also a loving friend of the poor drunkard, and would link his arm in his and take him home, and give him no rest, but go to his home time after time until he got him to the Mission Hall. The little children loved him very much. You would see them take his hand, and sometimes quite a little group would be gathered round him."

Mr. Kemp writes to Dr. Maxwell : " Mr. Callis's preaching was most definitely Christ *crucified* and *risen* again. There were two hymns he was very fond of in open-air services—' When I survey ' and ' Just as I am.' He used often to give out a verse or a line, and then speak on it ;

and so, all through the hymns, pleaded strongly
with souls. At the after meetings on Sunday
nights he would often stand with his eyes shut
for some time while he was speaking. Some of
his favourite verses were, 'Thou wilt keep him
in perfect peace,' etc., and 'Except the Lord
build the house,' etc. He was always ready to
help and sympathize, and his hearty hand-
shake was like his speaking. His death has
been the call to at least one to go forward to
the work."

At one time occupying two bright little rooms
in a quiet road, he thought them too luxurious
for a shepherd of the flock, so many of whom
were in such far humbler circumstances, and
having to endure the hardships of poverty ! He
accordingly changed his lodgings for rooms more
in the midst of the poorer people of the parish.
His health showing signs of giving way, he was
persuaded to return to his old quarters on higher
ground and in a purer atmosphere. It was
urged upon him that attention to health was an
important duty on the part of those who are
called to minister to others ; that he should try
and carry into the homes of poverty and the
sick chambers as much brightness as possible
even in his personal appearance. To neglect

health in work for God may be a temptation of the great adversary, aiming thereby at the laying aside of a disturber of his kingdom and an earnest worker for Christ.

The golden opportunities of the metropolis for sharing in great philanthropic and missionary enterprises were much valued and gladly embraced. At the same time he could not help expressing a wholesome fear lest his life should degenerate into a *rush*, with little power or comfort. He mentions at this time a visit of Dr. Lankester, C.M.S. physician, to the Monthly Gleaners' Meeting, and was much struck with a remark he made: "My Christian friends think me a fool for giving up my practice, while my unbelieving acquaintances all say that it is my plain duty, if my religion is real." All such episodes clearly told upon his mind in relation to his future. About this time he wrote a very touching letter to his father, expressing his fervent gratitude for all his great kindness and self-denial on his behalf. He adds: "I wish the son over whom you have spent so much were worthy of it," and then he adds solemnly: "We all need a living faith in the Holy Ghost and in God's power to keep. . . . I preached with a self-accusing conscience on God's Will 'our sanctification ' last Sunday morning. I long for a permanent experience of a life of holiness." The former movement of his mind towards the foreign mission field now became stronger. Sometimes old difficulties and perplexing questions cropped up again, which were discussed with his kind vicars, ever full of sympathy towards their ardent fellow-helper.

Chapter IV

"Recommended to the grace of God for the work."—*Acts*
xiv. 26.

IT was not until he had been nearly three
years at his curacy at Woolwich, that John
finally decided to offer himself to the Church
Missionary Society for the Uganda Mission. After
talking over with his vicar on several occasions
the question of the duty of every young man
to ascertain whether he were not called to the
foreign field, he went to the Society's house and
made the offer, saying that he might be rightly
charged with a want of sincerity if he continued
only to talk about the work.

One who had proved himself so devoted to
the service of Christ was readily accepted by
the Committee, and commended to the Lord in
prayer, led by one present (the Rev. F. Storer
Clark) who had known him from his earliest
days. He expresses in a letter at this time his

delight at the thought of being supported by
Norwich Gleaners.

In the month of March of that year, 1896, a
deep sorrow had befallen the family. The
youngest daughter, Monica Evelyn, a bright and
affectionate girl of sixteen, died, after a few days'
illness, at school at Eastbourne. The brother
went down from London on the receipt of the
news of her serious illness, but was too late, as
were her parents, to see her before she had
been called away. Her father was from home
in Northamptonshire at the time, attending his
own mother's funeral.

As the beautiful, lifeless form had to be removed as soon as possible, John travelled up
to London that night, and on to Norwich by
the first morning train, there to prepare for the
reception in the shadowed home. Again and
again did he steal into the drawing-room of
the old home, where it lay enclosed in the
oaken casket, covered with wreaths of fresh
spring flowers, but the thoughts, resolutions, and
prayers of the devoted brother in that silent
presence are known only to God. The sorrow
was deep indeed. John was often noticed, after
his return to Woolwich, even in church, to be
overwhelmed with grief.

Two days after the sister's funeral, the grand-mother on the maternal side was also called away, at the ripe age of ninety-seven. Thus from the family circle three were gone in ten days.

The decision for the mission field having been made, he wrote to his mother some weeks afterwards :—

"Your letter has just come, also a very kind one from Mr. Wilkinson (C.M.S. Secretary) by the same post. David's words, I Chron. xxix. 14, 15, brought home to me the other day the privilege of being allowed to give to God. He will, I am sure, heal the very bitter smart of parting from one another. Darling Monica's early home-call emphasized the fact that we are only strangers and pilgrims here, and that true lasting fellowship with one another belongs to the future." The words of the passage referred to are deeply impressive, almost pro-phetic, to those he has left to mourn his loss. "Who am I, and what is my people, that we should be able to offer so willingly after this sort? for all things come of Thee, and of Thine own have we given Thee. For we are strangers before Thee, and sojourners, as were all our fathers : our days on earth are as a shadow, and there is none abiding."

The May Meetings, which proved to be the last he attended, were, this year, of very special interest to him. Mr. G. L. Pilkington — now, alas ! also fallen in the field—and the Rev. G. K. Baskerville both gave a glowing account of Uganda and its people, and the blessing which was attending the work there. John was much drawn to both these devoted missionaries. Mr. Pilkington remarked to him that, so great was the interest of the missionary's life in Uganda, if he went out, he would never wish to retire from it. This, no doubt, influenced him much in deciding to join the mission in that fair and promising field. From all accounts it seemed, moreover, to be just the climate to suit his constitution, and to give him the prospect of a long and useful life in God's service in Central Africa. The offer to the C.M.S. was made in June, and, on acceptance, he found that he must be prepared to sail with the next party for Uganda in the following September.

The dismissal of the Uganda party of 1896 took place July 23rd, at the lower room of Exeter Hall. The Rev. H. E. Fox introduced the missionaries, who were seated on the platform, by name, adding a few particulars about each. Coming to J. S. Callis, he spoke of him as "a

Cambridge man with an Oxford polish," because
of his having gone, after taking his degree at Cambridge, to Wycliffe Hall, Oxford, for special preparation for Holy Orders. Several of the outgoing
missionaries addressed the meeting. Mr. Pilkington's words will now have a special interest, as
his career of noble service has so suddenly closed.
"He hoped," he said, "before he saw their faces
again, to be present at another dismissal—a dismissal in Uganda of missionaries from the Waganda to the nations round them and to those
on the coast. When this came about, there
would be, not merely the moral effect of the
addition of new workers, but the testimony of a
new nation, African and not English, from the
interior and not from beyond the sea. Then
how grand it would be if they could advance
down the Nile Valley. The way was already or
would be open as far as Wadelai. If you want
to evangelize the Soudan," he cried, "reinforce
Uganda." To this magnificent prospect he added
an appeal for prayer, especially for the native
Church. "Every face here," he said, "means a
heart, which means prayer." Then followed the
committee's instructions to the missionaries. They
were of an unusually solemn and impressive
character, the keynote being given in the open-

ing words—death before life, humiliation before
victory, the cross before the crown ; " Except
a corn of wheat fall into the ground and die, it
abideth alone ; but if it die, it bringeth forth
much fruit." They were reminded that in
West Africa fifty-three missionaries, men and
women, laid down their lives for Christ in the
first twenty years. So, in East Africa, fifty-two
years have elapsed since Johann Ludwig Krapf,
the very first missionary in the land to which
they were going, after laying the frail body of
his young wife in her grave on the mainland
opposite Mombasa, wrote home the memorable
words : " As the victories of the Church are always
gained by stepping over the graves of her members, you may be sure that you are called to the
evangelization of East Africa." Again, returning to his work after his first visit home, he wrote :
" Our God bids us build a cemetery before we
build a church. The resurrection of East Africa
must be effected by our destruction. But the
chain of missions across the continent will yet
be completed when the Lord's hour is come."

The missionaries were urged to go forward to
their work, encouraged by the remembrance of
the great things God had done for the mission
before in such a spirit, and which had cost so

many precious lives since Krapf's time. They must ever let their message be the message of the cross, and never be ashamed to confess and preach Christ crucified. They must be prepared for disappointments, for the death of many sanguine anticipations and even reasonable hopes. Not only in the work of Christ, not only in the work of His servants, but in the hearts and lives of His servants themselves, death must precede life. If faithful to Christ, they were further reminded of the promise which they could claim for themselves : " When Christ, who is our life, shall be manifested, then shall ye also with Him be manifested in glory." In conclusion, referring to the special cross some of them might have to bear in separation from those most dear to them, they were urged to carry it bravely and resolutely for Christ's sake, and in His strength—that Divine strength is made perfect in weakness—" He will not fail you, and He will not fail to recompense you."

The sight of that platform filled with those who had offered themselves for the cause of Christ in East Africa, and the deep solemnity which accompanied the proceedings on the occasion, could not but be deeply affecting to many, especially to those who were parting with those so dear to them. Two, at least, upon that "altar" were going out, soon to be called to a higher service, but never to see their native land again —Pilkington and Callis. The latter's father, with whom at the time there was something of a pre-sentiment that so it might be with him, on reaching home wrote the following lines :—

REINFORCEMENTS FOR UGANDA.

In Memoriam. July 23rd, 1896. Exeter Hall.

Showers of blessing have fallen of late
On Uganda's fertile soil ;
    White is that field,
    Abundant the yield,
The fruit of past labourers' toil.

The names of the sowers, whose work is done,
Called home to receive their hire,
    With fragrance fill
    The whole Church still,
And with zeal many hearts inspire.

These have heard the call to that harvest field
To be reapers for the Lord—
    A Sacrifice
    Bought with a price,
For the cause of His Holy Word.

They have counted the cost of severed ties
From home and from native land,
    And ready now
    For altar or plough,
In the presence of God they stand.

O Lord of the harvest, be with them all,
Give Thy cause in their hands success,
    That we and they
    At close of day
Thy Holy Name may bless.

Thy Grace sufficient be their supply,
Thy Love their sustaining power ;
    Their eye of faith
    In life or death
See Thee present every hour.

The call comes still
From that distant land.
Does it not come to thee ?
    Who will say " No " ?
    Who, " I will go " ?
" Lord, if Thou wilt, send me ! "

John was now busy in making the needful preparation for the long journey. Having concluded
his work at All Saints', Woolwich, in August he
joined his family at Felixstowe for a few weeks'
rest and change. From this place he wrote to
the compiler of this memoir, in reply to a letter
expressing prayerful good wishes for him in his
future work : " Prayer and Christian sympathy are
the only things that seem valuable at this time.
. . . Thank you much for the prayers which
I know you have offered as my godfather. It
was not until 1889, when an undergraduate, that
it pleased the Lord to convert me. I owe so
much, under God, to the prayers of my parents

4

and, I feel, of yourself also, during the years when I cared for none of these things."

At Felixstowe, as elsewhere, he found opportunities of doing something for the great cause to which he had now devoted his life. Children's services were being conducted upon the beach, and he was asked to take part in them. On one occasion, with a large map of Africa hung upon poles on the sand, and with a few pictures and curios, he gave an account of the people and customs of the country to which he was going, and was listened to with marked attention by his youthful hearers.

He also preached in his brother-in-law's church at Walton, and spoke at a missionary meeting held in the Vicarage garden. The meeting was a somewhat remarkable one. Other speakers were Dr. Harford Battersby, from West Africa; the Rev. P. G. Wood, formerly curate of Holy Trinity, Norwich, and afterwards missionary in Cairo; and the Rev. W. H. M. Aitken, who said that he wanted one letter to be a missionary—he was only a "*missioner*," but he had been privileged, by his parochial mission work at home, to be the means of influencing many to give themselves to the work in the *foreign* mission field.

In July John went with his brother-in-law

to the Keswick Convention. He had been on a former occasion with his vicar, Mr. Rice, and had found it a time of refreshing. Of the last visit the Rev. E. Symonds writes: " He was not by any means one of those who thought that the attendance at a convention was a *sine quâ non* to a healthy spiritual state. In fact, his nature inclined him to the opposite view—that a man learned more by individual dealing and communion with God alone than by attending large gatherings of the convention type. All the more noticeable that he should have been found at Keswick. When there, it was by no means his habit to attend one meeting after another in the course of the day, but rather to be content with two or three, and to spend the time between in quiet thought over what he had heard, and in quiet enjoyment of the beautiful scenery which gives the charm to Keswick. I often recall his words, ' There stand the mountains '—he meaning to imply that, in spite of all men might *think* and *say* about Divine truth, it still existed, and was, in fact, as immovable as Skiddaw above us. Our talk ended with the subject of the glory of the Lamb, as recorded in the Book of Revelation (chap. v.). He had lately been studying Wordsworth's *Lectures on the*

Apocalypse, and was very full of the subject. I little thought, when a month later he preached for the first and last time in my church, and chose, at my request (made whilst on Derwentwater together), Revelation v. 6 as his text, that he himself would so soon be singing the new song. But God has so willed it."

At the end of August the family returned to Norwich. On the 30th John preached farewell sermons in his father's church of Holy Trinity (South Heigham). He addressed the children in the afternoon from St. John vi. 9, "What a lad can do." In the evening there was a large congregation, to hear the last sermon of the young missionary before his departure from home. The text chosen seems now prophetic. It was St. John xii. 24, "Except a corn of wheat fall into the ground and die, it abideth alone; but if it die, it bringeth forth much fruit." With intense earnestness, as was his wont, the preacher dwelt upon the importance of death to the world and sin in those who would give themselves to Christ, and be used by Him in His service. Such is the condition of great fruitfulness unto God. Those who would bring forth much fruit must be prepared to die, as the Lord Himself was.

An after-meeting was held, to which nearly

all stayed. The venerable Canon Patteson, who had given a daughter to the mission-field in China, also early called home, concluded the solemn service with a fervent commendatory prayer and pronounced the Benediction.

The parishioners took a deep interest in one whom they had known from his early days going from their pastor's home into the great mission-field of Central Africa, and constantly made kind inquiry as to his welfare to the end of his brief missionary career.

Thus the last Sunday in England ended. He went up to London on the following Tuesday to make final preparations for the journey, and to take leave of his friends at Woolwich. On the evening of September 1st, he was warmly welcomed at a large gathering for tea in the Mission Hall. Later in the evening he gave some account of the missionary work in Eastern Africa, to enable his old friends the better to follow him in thought to the sphere of labour which had opened to him, asking the prayers of all for a safe journey and a blessing on the work in Uganda.

Then followed an interesting item in the proceedings. The Rev. J. W. Morris (the vicar) had been asked to present to him an illuminated

address from the parishioners and members of
the congregation, together with a purse of £40.
He spoke in kindly and grateful terms of the
association of the departing missionary in the
work of the Church and parish since the time he
succeeded the Rev. the Hon. W. Talbot Rice as
vicar, and expressed the fervent wish of all that
he might be greatly blessed in his future work.
The gift was received by John with warm expressions of thanks to the vicar, and to all with
whom he had been so happily associated in the
Lord's work during the three years of his curacy
amongst them.

The address was as follows :—

" *To the Reverend John Samuel Callis, B.A.*

"We whose names appear below beg your acceptance
of the accompanying purse of money, as a token of our
love and esteem, on the occasion of your leaving the parish
of All Saints', Plumstead, wherein you have faithfully
laboured for the last three years.

" During that time you have indeed made your influence
felt, and your example of self-denial, together with your
whole-hearted Christian zeal, will long be remembered.
Unwillingly we say good-bye, but earnestly do we wish you
joy and blessing in your new sphere of work, and we will
not forget to pray that you may be the means of winning
souls to Christ in that part of the foreign Mission field
to which you have been called by your Heavenly Father.

"ALL SAINTS',"
      "*September*, 1896."

(*Here follow the names.*)

Amongst those present on this deeply interesting occasion was the Rev. Andrew Jukes, author
of several valuable theological works. Mr. Jukes'
friendship and fatherly counsel had been very
highly esteemed by the young curate during his
ministry in the parish, and had been a very
great help to him. The venerable theologian
spoke of him in the most affectionate terms. Dr.
Maxwell, another warm friend of John's, and formerly Medical Missionary in Kashmir, was also
present, and expressed the same kindly feeling
towards him and admiration of his course in the
curacy of the parish.

On the following evening, his last in England,
he preached at All Saints' Church, in which a
large congregation assembled to hear his farewell sermon. He spoke most earnestly upon the
words, "Father, glorify Thy name" (St. John xii.
28), reminding his hearers that it was the will of
the Father that His Name should be glorified in
the *death* of the Son, and again dwelling much
upon the 24th verse,—the text of his sermon at
Norwich,—"Except a corn of wheat," etc.

September 3rd, the day of departure, had at
length arrived. One more brief visit was paid
to the schools to say a last good-bye to the
teachers and the dear children, who repeated to

him Psalm cxxi., " I will lift up mine eyes unto the hills," etc. He took leave of his mother and sister at the Liverpool Street Station Terminus, his father and Miss B—— going down to the steamer at Tilbury with him. With evident deep feeling, but with calm self-possession, he took a last leave of his father and the one whom he looked forward so hopefully to welcome to Africa, there to share his home and work. Mounting the highest deck, John with other missionary brethren and sisters stood waving their handkerchiefs to those on the boat as it receded towards the landing-place. So full of bright hope did the young missionary take his departure for his distant post of labour, and so full of hope were those most dear to him on earth that he would be spared many years to do, it might be, a great work for the Lord of the harvest in that most promising field, that they little thought it would be permitted them to see his face no more in this life.

Chapter V

"Let patience have her perfect work, that ye may be
perfect and entire, wanting nothing."—*James* i. 4.

THUS, as we have said—full of bright hope
and happy resolve—John Samuel Callis set
sail for his far-off missionary post in the Dark
Continent. There came from him, a few hours
after his start, a final loving message to his father :
" Thank you for all you have done in helping
me to come abroad. You will, I'm sure, never
regret it, nor my dearest mother. At present I
don't realize what leaving England means, but it
will all be paid back tenfold, whatever it costs.
I trust dear mother will be much strengthened
and blessed at this time." Very interesting details of the voyage reached England, as there
was opportunity of writing. The passengers on
board ship included a small party of " fellow-
workers unto the kingdom of God "—those men-

tioned in the preceding chapter, Miss Taylor,
Miss Timpson, and others. He was thus able to
enjoy much sweet fellowship with friends in
Christ like-minded with himself. The sights and
sounds of a long sea voyage, new to his experience, were full of interest to him. He writes
enthusiastically of the deep blue waters of the
Mediterranean crested with snow-white foam, of
the reading on deck at night by the electric light
to the sound of the sea all around, amidst the re-
volving lights of lighthouses peering through the
dark. A considerable portion of his time was
taken up with learning the language of Uganda
from Mr. Baskerville, of whom he speaks in the
warmest terms as a " dear, whole-hearted, affectionate fellow, full of faith, and therefore full of zeal
and of the Holy Spirit," and as " one who knows
much of the needs of Africa." Over and over again
in his letters he expresses the utmost anxiety to
use all spare moments in " waiting upon the Lord
for His power for work in that country." In a
letter to Miss B—— he says, " Pray for me about
the language ; at present it does seem so difficult
and I do want to speak soon. God used to give
His servants the gift of tongues, and He will not
fail to help now " ; and in a letter to his father, " I
want it to be a time of quiet tarrying upon God

for power from on high for work. I feel so helpless in some respects, not naturally having much
inclination for building and other arts useful to
a pioneer Missionary. I long above all things
for spiritual power—what Uganda and the rest
of the world wants above all things." It is interesting to read how every day opened with Bible
readings on the Epistle to the Hebrews, and closed
with hymns and prayer ; how one night the little
Missionary band sang hymns in a corner of the
deck in the dark, and prayed for all they loved
at home (of these he touchingly remarks elsewhere, "Our love to Christ, at Whose bidding we
go, makes not our love to them less strong. I
thank God it was hard to leave England, and
I thank Him for each one of those who *made* it
hard to leave the earthly Homeland"); how the
phrase "ocean of Thy love" in the well-known
evening hymn seemed clothed with almost a new
meaning in presence of the sea extending "wide
as the eye could travel, and, further, so deep, and
upholding the ship on its bosom—a graphic type
of the fulness of God's love." "May we," he
adds, "bathe in it, and have our hearts filled
with it, as He means us to do."

The writer again remarks, "I am trying to get
more time with God early in the morning. It

does bring blessing to have a tarrying time with Him, free from hurry, before all the rushing about begins and mixing with other people." But, while his whole heart was evidently thus given to God and to the work before him, it is refreshing to see how full he was of buoyant animal spirits, and how thoroughly he could enter into and partici-pate in the pleasures and enjoyments of others. He gives an amusing and graphic account of leap-frog and cricket on deck, and such-like de-vices for breaking the monotony of a long voyage. His religion was no morose, unsociable thing. It was a religion brim-full of sympathy, and quick to claim its share in all innocent pleasure. This his fellow-passengers seem to have fully recog-nised, if we are to judge from the hearty send-off they gave the missionary party when they left the ship at Aden. The first glimpse of Africa, sighted on the 15th, stirred up strong emotions in his heart. He rushed on deck. The grim and rugged coast of Morocco, seen in the distance, was a call to prayer and to renewed determina-tion, by God's grace, "not to know anything" among the peoples of the Dark Continent "save Jesus Christ, and Him crucified." He used after-wards always to sit on that side of the boat and work at Luganda.

A very happy time was spent at Malta. The party, on reaching Valetta, were met by Miss Lytton, who works among the British soldiers there. She offered her services as guide, and invited them to tea at the Presbyterian Army Chaplain's house. She had arranged a Missionary meeting afterwards, at which the soldiers and their friends might come together and wish them God-speed. John thus describes the arrival : "After much excitement amongst the brown-faced boat-men, we all 'escaped safe to land,' as St. Paul and his fellow-voyagers did long ago, a few miles up the shore." After the party had paid visits to many places of interest, Mr. Murray welcomed them to tea, and presided subsequently at the meeting, where all experienced much blessing. " It was good," John writes, "to find many simple loving Christians in a city of priests and processions. . . . It is impossible to describe the warmth and kindness of our Maltese friends. The happy hours will not be forgotten by us." At midnight they sailed away for Brindisi.

Port Said was reached on the 19th. The heat was very great, and it became necessary to sleep on deck, " in spite of the rats which manœuvre there when all is comparatively quiet." Aden was reached on the 22nd. John writes from here :

"Such a strange scene! Water-carts drawn
by camels, natives of all shades of brown and
black, bright-eyed boys begging and laughing full
of fun and mischief. The boy element seems to
prevail in Aden. On our anchoring, they came
out in canoes, swimming and diving for silver
coins. Every black man or boy has become an
object of deep interest to me. May the Lord give
me deep love for their souls. . . . We are
really making headway with the language—praise
Him, and go on praying." At Aden the missionary party had to leave the *Khedive* and
go on board the British India Company's ship
Canara. The passengers and ship's officers of
the *Khedive*, who had all shown a kindly interest
in them, crowded to watch them steam away in
the launch, which they did singing the Doxology.
But as they were not to start until the next
day, they went ashore, and drove in five broken-
down vehicles to the celebrated "Tanks." John
writes: "We passed on the way flocks of sheep
and goats, water-sellers, camels, and many Eastern
common objects which recalled the parables and
scenes of Scripture. The Tanks were wonderful
in their capacity for holding rain-water, which only
falls once in three years. To the wonderment of
our Mohammedan guides we sat by one of the

highest tanks and sang two hymns, 'Like a river glorious,' and 'Abide with me.'" The next day (the 23rd) they began the last part of their voyage, and reached Mombasa on October 1st. John remarks here, "On October 1st, 1888, I began my undergraduate life at Cambridge ; on October 1st, 1891, I began life in London as a Lay-Worker under Mr. Webb-Peploe ; on October 1st, 1896, I land in Africa."

An enthusiastic reception awaited them. As soon as the anchor was dropped, boats put off both from Mombasa and Frere Town containing brethren and friends eager to give them a hearty welcome. Dr. Baxter was one of the first. He had been working hard to collect porters, sheep, goats, donkeys, chairs for the ladies, for the journey up country. Very touching was the meeting between Mr. Baskerville and some of his Baganda boys, who had been left by him at Frere Town a year ago. They rushed into the water, flinging their arms round his neck, and showing every token of the warmest love. The Frere Town Boys' Band gave the missionaries a rough but hearty serenade. The beach was covered with men, women, and children, who had come to see them. It was a great treat also to meet with Bishop Tucker, and to go with him to the new

church for a short, simple, but very real service
of thanksgiving for journeying mercies. This
church had been built entirely by native Christians. It is seated with pews of teak wood. The
pulpit, reading-desk, and lectern would be quite
worthy of an English church. The walls are very
thick, and a number of doors are placed along each
side of the building, as well as at the west end,
thus providing excellent ventilation. A glad and
happy day indeed was John's first Sunday in
Africa. At first it was suggested that the missionary party should have an English Communion
Service, but, instead of that, they joined the native
Christians at their service at 9 a.m. The church,
which holds a congregation of 350, was full. The
Rev. H. K. Binns, who is the senior Missionary at
the Coast, and has been in the locality for more
than twenty years, preached fluently in Swahili to a
most attentive audience from 1 Corinthians xv. 22,
23. The hymns were sung most lustily. They
were translations of well-known English hymns
sung to the old tunes. John remarks : " It is wonderful to hear these Christians sing their Swahili
hymns. We just know enough Luganda to be
able to pronounce the words. They are written in
Roman characters, so *we* sing also, though not
much ' with the understanding ' as yet. When

the general congregation had withdrawn, there
followed the Holy Communion, and sweetly and
powerfully was their nearness in Christ with those
dear people, rescued from heathenism and slavery,
realized ! Yes, "Christian fellowship is felt to be
a very real thing out there!" Two days after
(October 6th) came the Dedication Service of the
new church. This had been postponed on account
of the Bishop having been in Uganda. All the
clergy and ladies from the neighbouring Missions
were present. John shall give the story of the
day's proceedings in his own words : " It is almost
impossible to describe the heartiness and reality of
the Dedication Service. It was also the Harvest
Festival. The Bishop was met at the west door
by four C.M.S.. clergymen and the native pastor
(the Rev. I. M. Semler). Mr. Binns preached, and
the Bishop took the Holy Communion Service.
The church was filled to overflowing with a very
reverent congregation, who joined in the service
and sang heartily. Many brought offerings of
fruit. In the afternoon, at 3 p.m., a Confirmation
Service was held. The Bishop gave the addresses,
and Mr. Binns translated. The Bishop read
the Service in Swahili. It was, again, a most
impressive sight to see thirty young men and
young women, gathered from heathenism, volun-

5

tarily confirming the promises of their baptism.
Three of Mr. Baskerville's boys from Uganda were
amongst the number. These went up last, the
Bishop reading the words in Luganda." Whilst at
Frere Town John lodged with Mr. Binns—a man
(to his mind) the ideal of a missionary, good at
everything—carpentering, building, tinkering, etc.,
and a most earnest and effective preacher. It was
felt by him to be a great privilege to be spending
his waiting time with such charming people. He
speaks with enthusiasm also of the place. The
scenery is splendid, the flowers glorious—hibiscus,
oleander, etc., tall palm trees with their clusters of
cocoa-nuts everywhere, vegetable and animal life
abounding, the morning and evening tints most
beautiful, the sea and cliffs, all these combining to
make a perfect picture. But chiefly, Frere Town
is a bright spot morally—a sort of oasis in the
spiritual desert of heathenism and Mohammedanism. It is a great centre for missionaries, several
ladies and men working in the Freed Slaves'
Schools. The Frere Town boys are bright, and
some of them quick at lessons. They do the cooking (and very well too), and are most anxious to
help in any way. Men and boys alike are courteous and obliging ; but the women and girls are
far behind, seeming coarser and ill-mannered.

This, doubtless, arises from their bringing up, Africa's women having been in the past treated more like dogs than human beings. There is a Divinity college in Frere Town in the charge of the Rev. J. E. Hamshere. It is for training young men to be school teachers, and for the ministry. The students are bright, earnest men. Filled with the Spirit of God, they will exert an incalculable influence for good. Africa must be evangelized by Africans. The European work is to train and feed the teachers.

Frere Town is a great contrast to Mombasa, which is bigoted and desperately ignorant—noise, dirt, and Mohammedanism being its principal characteristics. Very few visible results have so far crowned the work of Missions there. John describes his walk through the town with the Rev. W. C. Taylor, whose courteous manner and sympathy, he thinks, must win the people from their bigotry. " We came to a house where, amid much shouting, and dancing, and drum-beating, an evil spirit was being exorcised. Mr. Taylor told the exorciser that he was a self-deceiver, and also deceiving the people. The crowd became rather angry, and said 'Bwana Taylor' lied. They all seemed to know him." Two afternoons a week open-air services are held in the Market Place.

During this waiting time our young missionary
occupied himself most diligently in learning Luganda, and in helping forward the arrangements
for the caravan. He was ' longing to be on the
tramp." In a letter to his father, alluding to the
dear people in South Heigham being divided in
opinion about his coming, he says: "Tell them,
with my Christian love, that I am not at all
divided in my own mind on the subject. I think
it was Krapf (I saw his wife's grave on Saturday)
who said, ' The cry of Christendom is but a faint
echo of the cry of Heathendom.' The need of
men in nominally Christian lands is great, but that
of Africa is infinitely greater. I hope they will all
pray earnestly and *constantly* for us who are in
Africa for Christ. I shall make a point of remembering the last Sunday in the month, when you
have the Missionary Prayer Meeting in church."
In the same letter he writes of the possible
dangers on the route to Uganda from lions, and
tells of one of Mr. Roscoe's boys who ventured
outside his camp tent one night without a light.
Though he was only four yards away, a lion
sprang upon him, and the poor fellow was carried
off. He was a bright Christian lad. He adds sig-
nificantly, after detailing the precautions which
would be taken by the missionary band, "The

God of Daniel still can shut the mouths of lions."
Very interesting was it to hear that a Confirmation had just been held there, at which there were
350 candidates, most of whom had been baptized
by Mr. Fitch. The work of Mr. Fitch and his
sister was, by universal testimony, most thorough.

The difficulties in the way of making a start
for the front lasted six weeks. John aptly remarks : " The time of waiting at the coast has been
a time of learning patience. We came out longing
to begin our march at once, and we have been
kept waiting. We long to get where we are to
teach, but we are delayed here to *learn*." In a
letter to Miss Durnford, a Plumstead friend, he
writes : "Delays seem quite the rule in Africa,
and we have need of patience. . . . I am
finding in this tarrying time that God is *before*
and *behind* as well as *in* us. After all, He
wants *ourselves* more than our work." The for-
warding in advance of the necessary supplies,
and the deluges of rain which fall in November,
combined to make a forward movement at once
impossible. It is deeply interesting to note how
precious experience in missionary work came
out of the enforced delay. We read of moonlight
meetings arranged for the natives by Mr. Binns,
at which each missionary spoke " by interpre-

tation." It fell to John to address a meeting for all the Christian "native workers"—Sunday-school teachers, Church elders, Sunday after-noon visitors, etc. About forty-five came to tea, at Mrs. Binns' invitation. During tea, Miss Taylor, one of the Uganda ladies, sang to them. After the tea, partaken of in European style, John spoke on the Lord's commission to St. Peter, "Feed My lambs." "It was a joyful privilege," he writes, "to speak 'in the Name' to these fellow-labourers."

Then followed a most profitable and happy Saturday and Sunday at Kilindini, a suburb of Mombasa Town. John was the guest of the Rev. F. Burt, missionary in charge of the Mombasa mission work. Kilindini is situated about two miles from Mombasa Town. The barracks in which the Indian soldiers are stationed are there. It is also the starting point of the Uganda railway. John's object in going to Kilindini was to attend a Baptismal Class on the Saturday evening. He says: "How can I describe the scene when we arrived! The meeting place is known among the missionaries as 'Kilindini Cathedral.' It is open at the west end, no wall or doors. The thatch comes down low, as in most African buildings. It is seated with trunks of trees lying one behind the other. When we arrived, five men were sitting on the men's side and about twenty-five women opposite. One lamp was burning, and the native catechist, Levi, in his snow-white long garment, was speaking from a rough reading-desk. After prayer Mr. Burt gave his instruction as to the meaning of baptism and what it involved. To see these ignorant, low-born men and women just beaming with the joy of the Holy Spirit was a sight worth taking the whole journey from England to behold." These people were not Mombasa people, but had settled on the island from the mainland. Some of the men preparing for baptism were at that time "on safari," *i.e.* gone up country as porters for caravans. The hour spent in "Kilindini Cathedral" was an hour never to be forgotten. On the Sunday John helped Mr. Burt at the English Holy Communion Service, held at 7.30 in the ground-floor room in the ladies' house. He took a lads' Bible Class in the ladies' house, at Miss Grieve's invitation. She interpreted. The lads are "house-boys" in the houses of Europeans, many of them brought up at Frere Town or at other mission stations. They are mostly baptized, but the persecution they meet with in Mombasa Town makes it hard for them to hold fast their profession. They are argued with by bigoted

Mohammedans, and insulted by other lads. A favourite sneer is to call them "black Europeans." Eleven came to the class, which was fewer than usual on account of the rain, and rain in Africa means something a great deal more than rain in England! The subject taken at the class was the choice of Moses (Heb. xi.), what he "refused" and what he "chose." Next followed the English service, held in the Custom House. Besides the missionaries seven others attended, among them four Eurasians who had come from India to serve as clerks in the railway works. John speaks of the joy he felt in reading the full evening service for the first time since leaving England. There was a solemn appropriateness to his own case, as God's providence subsequently ordered, in the subject chosen for the address. He spoke, from St. John iii. 30, of St. John the Baptist as merely "a *voice* of one crying"— "bearing witness" to the Word. The "*voice*" was soon to be silenced, but "*the Word*" is eternal and must increase. After the service he went with Mr. and Mrs. Burt to pay their weekly visit at the old Portuguese fort, now used as a jail. About ten prisoners were together in large locked rooms. The poor fellows crowded to the barred doors at Mr. Burt's voice. John stayed

at one door with Mrs. Burt while her husband
went to another cell. "It was a picture," he
says, "to watch her speaking fluently in Swahili
to these men—just speaking to them simply of
Christ. Surely such work must *tell*, and win
them (D.G.) to that true 'Prophet that should
come' (and has come and will come) into the
world. They did not attempt to argue, they
only looked earnestly at Mrs. Burt and said,
'True, true,' again and again." John added a
few words by interpretation. "When these
Mohammedans return to their homes, they will
not forget that it was the Christian who visited
them whilst suffering for their misdeeds." Sunday
night brought another new experience — the
Mission Service at the Mission Hall. After Mr.
and Mrs. Burt had spoken, John was called upon to
address the company. Of this and other opportunities, he writes : "What a joy in the middle of
a Mohammedan town to witness for Christ! It
is difficult to describe what it is to preach Christ
out here. The little foretaste I have had makes
me long to know the language better and get
to work." He adds some interesting remarks
about the Mohammedans generally. They are
particularly bigoted and conceited. Whilst
friendly to the missionaries, they tell them plainly

that they are certain they are right and the missionaries wrong. One of them said to Mr. Burt, "Jesus, the Son of Mary, was a great and good Prophet, but God forbid that I should say He was the Son of God." They rely upon their works, prayers, and faith in Mahomet. The crowning sin in their eyes is to disbelieve in God's prophet. Any sin against morality is nothing in comparison with this. Consequently the work in Mombasa is slow. Still, the earnest looks and attention of hearers give hope that the seed is taking root, and that, in due time, there will come a harvest. It is thought that there are several secret believers, and that, if *one* would but lead the way by coming to baptism, many more would follow. *One* baptism would be like setting a light to a ready-laid fire. John remarks at this point that the "Slave Question" is a *very* large one, and that it seems difficult to know what would happen if the large number of women and girls were suddenly freed. The case of domestic slavery is very different from what we generally know in England as "slavery."

Here is a brief epitome of the life of the missionaries in Frere Town. A daily Prayer Meeting was held at noon. This included a ten minutes' address, taken by each in turn. Every Wednes-

day night, at 7.30, a Bible Reading was held for
an hour and a half. Once a month a Gleaners'
Union Meeting took the place of this. The missionaries from Mombasa came across for these
weekly meetings in boats rowed by strong mission
boys. John cheerily concludes his circular letter
thus : " We shall, all well, spend our Christmas
in *tents*. We hope to be more than half-way
to Uganda. Several of our party have brought
Christmas puddings. Also, as several have guns,
we hope to have some game. This last item on
the menu is, however, uncertain at present, as our
sportsmen have not yet learned to shoot. After
shooting without success at a hawk which was
carrying off chickens, Mr. Wigram was reported
to have shot an owl. It was also reported that
the unfortunate bird was asleep at the time
sitting on a tree enjoying its afternoon siesta ! "

We next hear of John at Mzizima. This is
a Medical Mission Station, beautifully situated
amongst cocoanut palms within sight of Frere
Town. He had gone to pay a visit to Dr. and
Mrs. Edwards. The hospital service is conducted
by Mr. Burt, the patients consisting almost entirely of heathen and Mohammedans, with a very
small admixture of Christians sent from inland
mission stations. The time spent at Mzizima was

most enjoyable.   Mrs. Edwards had in her early
days been connected with St. Jude's, Mildmay,
and knew personally many of John's most valued
friends (such as the Rev. W. and Mrs. Penne-
father, Canon Garratt, and the Rev. W. Hay
Aitken), and had been thrown into company with
all sorts and conditions of Christians in different
parts of Europe.   They thus found that they
had much in common, and the intercourse was
the more delightful and helpful.

Mrs. Edwards, writing to his father after his
home call, says: "I cannot tell you what a pleasure
and refreshment his visit was to us.   We were
greatly struck with Mr. Callis's thoughtfulness and
singular maturity.   It was most evident that he
had been deeply taught by the Holy Spirit, and
his gentle humility and unobtrusiveness made
what he said all the more striking.   His thoughts
were evidently dwelling much on the life to come,
and he several times mentioned to me the loss of
a young sister, which led up to that subject.   One
felt how intensely *real* all was to him, and how
actually he was living in the presence of our Lord.
He spoke of a book of Mr. Jukes', 'The New
Man,' which had been a great help to him.   Just
before he left we took a short walk together.   A
little black boy had followed him from Frere

Town in the boat. He carried him most of the way home, because he thought he must be tired. I noticed his love for children, and sympathy for the weak. He was quite taken up with this little fellow, though they could not understand one another's language at all. It is a mystery why such a life has ended so early for the work here. One cannot understand, one can only trust the love that knows and orders all.

Whilst at Frere Town news came from the front which plainly showed how graciously God in His providence had been watching over our young missionary. The floods had been terrible. The Taru desert had become an inland sea, and the natives had taken to the trees, as their houses were under water. Five mail-men, bringing letters from Taita, had been drowned. "We can only be most thankful," he writes, "that we did not start in October. If porters had been available on landing, and if we had started, the rains and floods would almost have swamped us." He adds : "Looking through the past months I see God's hand leading very plainly, and I can but praise Him. Every one who comes to the mission field says it is *there* the Lord draws souls closer to Him-self, and I can only say, Amen. The waiting time has been a time of looking after our own vineyards."

Chapter VI

"Be strong and of a good courage : for the Lord thy God
is with thee whithersoever thou goest."—*Josh.* i. 9.

A T last came the long-desired signal to move.
The morning of Saturday, November 28th,
saw the missionary party, thirteen in number,
commencing their journey to Uganda. But first
came a happy gathering of all engaged in the
Lord's work in Mombasa and Frere Town at the
Lord's Table—a sweet but all too brief season of
"strengthening one another's hands in God." On
the beach they found almost all Frere Town
assembled to bid them God-speed. The head
engineer of the Uganda Railway had kindly
arranged for them to be taken by train to Mazeros
(fourteen miles from Mombasa). Crossing in the
mission boats from Frere Town, they were then
conveyed in curious little carriages, pushed by
hand, on railway-like lines to Kilindini, which has
been already mentioned as the terminus of the
new railway. Here is a large station-yard, marked

out by high iron railings, inside which are large
iron stores. Three engines are already working
on the line, and two more had come out in
sections by the last mail. The "Express" was
due to leave Kilindini at 10 a.m. sharp ; but, with
the punctuality usual in Africa, started at 11.45.
It consisted of an engine and two trucks—the first
of these seated with planks for the occasion—the
other filled with personal goods (which had to be
as few as possible, as many of the porters had
failed to put in an appearance) and with the
missionaries' "boys." These "boys" wait, cook,
wash up, and do all necessary work for their
masters. Loud cheers from the little knot of
Europeans, who had come down to see them
off, greeted the moment of departure. Slowly,
through lovely scenery, they travelled in the
direction of the narrow belt of water which
separates Mombasa from the mainland, and
crossed by the temporary bridge. Heavy showers
of rain came on, during which they lunched under
umbrellas and mackintoshes. About three miles
from Mazeros there had been a break-down on
the railway. Consequently the train could pro-
ceed no further. As it had to return at once,
loads were hastily deposited by the side of the
line, and a somewhat hurried but loving farewell

taken of the missionary brethren from the coast.
John feelingly speaks of this as "a small repeti-
tion of what he had gone through in September,
when bidding farewell to the dear, dear friends
in the Home country."

And now for a picture of daily camp life !
This memorable Saturday, at its close, finds the
missionary party for the first time under canvas—
each one having his own tent, bed, table, chair,
etc.   At 4 a.m. each morning, Dr. Baxter, leader
of the caravan, blows a horn to arouse every one—
missionaries and porters (of whom there are 200)
alike.   After packing up comes breakfast in the
open, whilst the tents are being taken down.   At
6 a.m. (sunrise), or a little before, the caravan
starts.   After three hours' march a halt is made
for rest and refreshment.   The "boys" bring up
kettles, and tea is provided.   In half an hour a
fresh move is made.   The ground covered each
day varies from ten to twenty miles, according to
circumstances.   Water supply, or the supply of
firewood available, generally settles where the next
camp is to be.   The day's march is usually finished
well before mid-day.   Tents are then pitched ; all
partake of food; there is bathing and change of
apparel.   The afternoons are spent in studying
Luganda under Mr. Pilkington's most able tui-

THE C.M.S. UGANDA PARTY, 1896

(Rev. J. S. Callis second from right, back row)

tion. There are prayers amongst the missionaries themselves before tea, and prayers conducted by Mr. Baskerville for the Baganda "boys" and porters after tea. The sun sets all the year round at 6 p.m., with little variation. At 9 p.m. the indefatigable Dr. Baxter again blows the horn—a signal for the porters to cease laughing and talking over their camp fires. John remarks about these porters, that they are mostly a very degraded set, having no idea of enjoyment beyond the gratification of their animal lusts and passions. Though they are thoroughly well treated as regards food and shelter, they often suffer terribly from bronchitis, dysentery, etc. Dr. Cook is their medical adviser, the missionaries being in charge of Dr. Baxter. He also blows a horn every evening, and those who are ill come to him for medicine. The caravan on the march is a strange sight. There are the travellers—the male portion clothed in flannel shirts, Kharki knickers, puttees and boots, and armed with umbrellas and water-bottles. A native drum is carried, to cheer up the porters by its beating. A herd of sheep and goats (gradually decreasing) forms part of the caravan. Fifty pack-donkeys carry some of the loads, and eight are reserved for riding. Then there are the "jinrickshas"—carriages drawn by men—for the

6

ladies. These are in John's special charge. As
they are somewhat like hansom-cabs, it is a comparatively easy matter to pilot them up hill and
down dale. Still, there are sometimes accidents.
He thus describes one. The caravan was passing
some large water-holes, dug out of the side of the
line (near Mazeros) for the use of the workmen,
when, owing to the slippery state of the road
through mud, the man between the shafts of one
of the jinrickshas lost his footing. He pitched
sideways into the hole, dragging the chair after
him. Happily, there was but little water in this
particular hole, and no harm was done.

On the march there was generally but scant
time for quiet reading and prayer. All the more
reason (our young missionary interjects) for prayer
at home !

At Mazeros there was an English service at
9.30, outside the bungalow of an Englishman and
his wife, who had been living there for some time.
There are many such in those parts left as
" sheep without a shepherd," and of whom generally the sad testimony has to be borne, " Out
here Englishmen have no morals." After the
service, John enjoyed a walk across beautiful hills
to Rabai with Drs. Baxter and Cook, and paid a
second visit to the Rev. A. G. and Mrs. Smith, the

successors of Mr. and Miss Fitch, of whose God-inspired work mention has been already made. They stayed on Sunday to the Swahili service. The sermon was preached by the Rev. W. H Jones, who went up country with Bishop Hannington at the time of his murder. Mr. Jones is a native clergyman, who has worked at Rabai for twenty-five years.

The next news from our young missionary comes in a letter to his mother, dated December 9th, from Ndi. The party were then a hundred miles from the coast, and had been most favoured in their journey. They had met with plenty of water and much grass. The " Taru desert," where the trees are usually bare and white, the ground without grass, and the road for sixty miles exposed to a scorching sun, was now providentially covered with grass and shaded by leafy trees. The heavy rains had been God's messenger before them, to make their way thus easy and prosperous. After eight days' incessant daily march they reached the Government station at Ndi, and looked forward to a Sabbath on the morrow and a short rest. They were all perfectly well and fit in every way The weather was delightfully cool, and they had now reached an altitude of nearly 2,000 feet above sea-level. John

describes himself "writing seated on a box outside my tent. It is past six, and night is fast
coming on. The mountain by our camp stands
ou against a blue cloudy sky lighted up with the
setting sun." Two days after came a fresh move.
Meanwhile, all, including the donkeys, had much
enjoyed the rest. Two missionaries from Taita
had walked twenty miles to see the party, one of
them being Mr. J. A. Wray. There was much
trouble at this time about the porters. The party
had thirty-eight Waganda porters who legally belonged to a man named Geinel at Kibwezi, a
place about seventy-eight miles up country. They
deserted from him, because of his cruel treatment.
Mr. Pilkington decided to make a special journey
on a bicycle to try and propitiate this man with
money. If he should not succeed, they would all
run away rather than join his caravan, dreading
the deadly vengeance he would be sure to wreak
on them, if he once got them within his grasp
again. John goes on to remark, "British rule is
a great blessing here. If these things go on now,
what must it have been before there was any
civilized power to control! The country is so
vast, it will take time to get everything in hand."
Speaking again of the climate, he says: "The
climate is delightfully cool, except from about 10

a.m. to 4 p.m. The thermometer is always high, but, somehow, we don't feel the heat. I had no idea the country was so very lovely here. We walk through lanes very much like what we have in England in the spring." Bicycling was a useful resource for some of the party. They used to go on in advance, and get into camp two or three hours before the caravan, and decide where the four messes and sets of tents were to be placed. When the caravan arrived, and meal-time was come, all would sit on chairs or boxes at the camp tables, and enjoy quite a sumptuous repast. Porridge, beef, mutton, goats' flesh (this was generally very tough), biscuits, corn-flour, jam, rice, dates, onions, tinned potatoes, tea, coffee, cocoa, etc., made up a good menu. The meal would be enlivened with spicy tales of Dr. Baxter's hunting experiences and narrow escapes.

By this time, thanks to the excellent tuition of Mr. Pilkington, John was able to speak a few sentences to the Waganda porters about the Gospel. There were 160 of them in all, including head-men and Askaris. The Askaris carry guns and bullet cartridges. They also superintend the putting up of tents, and keep order among the porters. John writes very enthusiastically of tramp life, though not unfrequently it was varied

with dangerous elements. Just before the party
reached Mt. Songolani—a transport station, consisting of wattled stores containing provisions,
etc.—they were all awoke one night by a great
shouting and hubbub from the porters. A lion
had suddenly appeared. It had crept silently to
the corner of the camp, and then pounced upon
a porter's tent, dragging it off into the jungle.
The porter happily escaped with only a blow
from the lion's paw on his head—an injury soon
put right by Dr. Baxter. Game in these parts is
commonly plentiful—partridges, guinea-fowl, hares,
etc. Giraffes, hyænas, antelopes, and zebras
abound. No villages were passed the whole way,
as the natives prefer to live away from the caravan route for fear of ill-treatment and robbery.

Every evening there was a camp-fire lesson in
Luganda for an hour. The language proved very
interesting, and further good progress was made
under Mr. Pilkington's teaching. On the 15th,
the camp was pitched at Kinani, and a splendid
view of Mt. Kilimanjaro greeted the travellers'
eyes. The two peaks were seventy-five miles
distant. The setting sun lit up the outline with
lines of gold. Snow lay here and there in patches
and creeks. Many of the porters climbed the
rocks to enjoy the view. The mountain is over

19,000 feet in height—3,000 feet higher than
Mt. Blanc. The summit was first reached by a
German a few years ago. The C.M.S. once had
a mission station on the side of the mountain, and
Dr. Baxter worked there. When Kilimanjaro
became German territory, the English Mission
withdrew, and the work is now carried on by a
German Lutheran Society.

About this time the missionary party crossed
their first river—the Tsavo. The current was swift,
and the water reached to the porters' waists. The
ladies were carried over in a chair, raised high by
six porters. The others were carried on porters'
shoulders, sitting with their knees on each side of
the head. The crossing took a considerable time,
as the donkeys had to be unloaded, and the
jinrickshas were very awkward to manage with
such steep banks. Ordinary streams were ridden
through on donkeys, if too deep to wade across.
The route now lay in a north-westerly direction,
and the altitude increased daily. An aneroid,
which had been presented to John by Mr. C. F.
Hinde, churchwarden of Holy Trinity, Heigham,
was found most useful in calculating this. A good
deal of anxiety was caused just then by the very
serious illness, from fever, of a lady who had come
with the caravan to rejoin her husband at Kikuyu.

But, with God's blessing on the skill of the two
doctors, and Miss Timpson (who is a fully qualified
nurse from Guy's), she recovered.

Christmas was now approaching, and our young
missionary's thoughts instinctively turned to home.
In a circular letter he says: " We shall share
with Christians at home the ' good tidings of great
joy,' which are *'for all people.'* We are here to
tell the Africans it is for *them."*

Sunday, the 20th, was spent at Kibwezi, where a
Scotch Industrial Mission is established. The
head of the Mission is now in Europe, and he
hopes to obtain leave to transfer the Mission to
another centre, as the natives have not come
to live round them, as they hoped would be the
case. The Wakamba, through whose territory
they were now journeying, are as yet untouched
by Christianity, no Europeans having yet learned
their language. Their country is vast and
mountainous. Until this year, the Kibwezi Mission has been the only attempt to reach this
tribe. None of the Scotch missionaries can yet
speak in their tongue, while the American "African
Inland Mission" was only started eighteen months
ago. The latter have a staff of fifteen male and
female missionaries, and several out-stations. But
they are heavily handicapped by having to form a

vocabulary and grammar. The Wakamba much resent the intrusion of white people into their country, and refuse to sell food to the missionaries or Government officials. They bring sugar-cane, curdled milk, cooking bananas into our camp, bartering them with the porters for beads, cloth, bottles, and salt. The Sunday at Kibwezi began with a celebration of Holy Communion at 7 a.m. in the rough grass and stake structure called "the Church." It was the first service held within any enclosure for some time. John had several very interesting talks with an English-speaking Hindoo clerk employed on the railway. This clerk read to him in his tent some excellent moral sayings from his Hindoo book of devotions—as to the shortness and uncertainty of life, and the need of turning to God at once. The most pathetic part was this : " There is no pleader, no pleader at all ; you must pray and pray, and do good." It was a great privilege to John to be able to tell him of the " One Mediator." He had been educated in a Government school in India, and he explained how, in the missionaries' schools in India, the Bible is taught, but in the Government schools there is no Bible. In the evening John wrote out several passages of Scripture, took them to the Hindoo's tent, and placed the Way before him clearly. He seemed to be longing for rest of soul, and the two had prayer together.

Illness amongst the party now made progress rather slow. One of the ladies was attacked with fever, and it took six hours to travel nine miles. On the 23rd Kiboko River was reached. The name means "Rhinoceros."

The country was full of wild animals. Hyænas approached the camp-fires, and roared with laughter, as though the camp had been pitched solely for their amusement. But they were not thought much of, any more than are the cats on the roofs at home. The bad water affected the health of two of the other ladies, and it was decided that a move on should be made without them, Dr. Baxter, Mr. Clayton, and John remaining behind in charge. The water is described as "just one dirty pool in the rocks." After tea, Mr. Clayton and John took their chairs to a far extremity of the camp, out of hearing of the invalids, and sang over the old, old Christmas hymns, "While shepherds watched," etc., "Hark! the herald angels sing," "O come, all ye faithful." They then read together the "Old, old story" in St. Luke ii., and the Epistle and Gospel for Christmas Day. After some prayer they felt that, though separated in body, the "joy" of the "good tidings" came fresh

to them, as to all the dear ones in the far-off homeland. The ladies were able to travel again at
night.

By 7.30 on Christmas morning the whole party
was re-united again at the Udiunzi River. Several
of the porters went on straight to Nzoi, where they
were to camp that night. John sought and
found rest and refreshment in the tent of the Rev.
H. W. Weatherhead, and arrangements were made
forthwith for a family-party Christmas dinner.
This was fixed for one o'clock, and was to be
preceded by a short service. The latter, however,
fell through, as the fatigue of the preceding night's
journey sent Dr. Baxter, Mr. Clayton, and John
into a sound sleep, and the others had to attend to
the invalid ladies. The boy cooks made a mistake in the hour and announced dinner at 11.45.
Soup, fish (sardines), venison, and a pudding given
to Mr. Weatherhead by a parishioner of St. George's,
Tufnell Park, corn flour, apple rings, and coffee,
made up the repast. Hymns succeeded, and Dr.
Baxter led in prayer. A start was made for Nzoi
at 3.15. On the way John saw what he describes
as "the most glorious sight he had ever seen."
The sun was setting behind Kilimanjaro, which
was covered with snow and ice. It would be impossible (he says) to paint adequately its beauty

and loveliness. The larger peak was visible, like a monster teacup reversed, and the sun threw an edging of gold all along the snow-line. The natives call the mountain "the abode of the gods," and it is certainly more celestial than earthly in its appearance. He sat on, watching the sun sinking behind the mountain, and then pressed forward, expecting to reach the camp immediately. But Christmas Day was not to end as happily as it began. After walking about three-quarters of a mile, he found himself under a lofty hill on the right, and about 500 yards from a river on the left. It grew dark fast, and he was clearly on the wrong path. He stood still and shouted. Presently voices came from the distance, only to die away, as some of the porters crossed the ford of the river, and went on to camp. It was now quite dark, except for the feeble light of a few stars, and he began to look out for a tree in which to spend the night. At last his shouts were heard. Shouting each moment, and waiting for the answer, he went straight for the river through reeds higher than his head. Three or four Askaris were in the river bed, and presently the headman of the caravan, who, on hearing the shouting, had turned back, piloted him another three miles or more, and he reached the camp safely at eight.

The Sunday following was spent by the missionary party with some missionaries of the "African Inland Mission" at Kerungu. They were hospitably entertained by Mr. and Mrs. Allen. A celebration of Holy Communion, with an address from Mr. Clayton, and hymns, hallowed the day. Heavy showers fell later on—so heavy that, at night, tents began to collapse. The Askaris and "boys" were some distance off, and the tents came tumbling down, leaving the occupants exposed to the full fury of the pitiless rain. Next day they marched along the bed of a river or mountain torrent. They had to cross and re-cross very often, now and then striking across the country to cut off corners where the channel was winding. Firewood was very scarce, and had to be bought from the Wakamba. A small quantity was purchased from a woman for an empty lime-juice bottle.

At length, on December 30th, they reached Machakos, and were regaled with tea and sugar, and milk from the real cow, after drinking from a "tin" cow for weeks. Machakos is a Government fort, and it was refreshing to see the British Protectorate flag waving over it. This is a blue flag with the Royal Standard at one corner, and the Lion Rampant towards the end. There are

several native houses in Machakos inhabited by
Swahili, and the place seems quite civilized. The
Wakamba are very restless at present, and have
had to be taught some severe lessons. They have
murdered fifteen sentries, and have attacked the
fort as late as five months ago. What they need
is a strong Mission to be started among them.
They are only one out of the many large tribes in
Africa who have never had a chance of hearing
and receiving the Gospel. Mr. Baskerville holds
out hopes that Baganda teachers may be sent out
to the Wakamba at some day not far distant.
These would pick up the language more quickly
than Europeans, and, being more intelligent than
the Wakamba, might, by God's blessing, become
first-rate teachers.

On January 6th the party reached Kikuyu, 350
miles from the coast, the " half-way house " to
Uganda, and received a hearty welcome from the
three Englishmen at the Fort. On the way they
passed over the shoulders of several very high hills
looking down over miles of plain. This vast tract
of perfectly level country was uninhabited, and
formed a kind of play-ground for antelopes and
wild beasts. The river Athi flows near, and the
Athi plain was shortly to be apportioned out to
English colonists on application to the Govern-

ment authorities. Before many years the plain would probably be studded with the homesteads of European settlers, and golden corn wave in all directions. It had been calculated that three crops of corn could be obtained in the course of one year. Here was obtained a splendid view of the two mountains—Kilimanjaro and Kenia. The latter was a fresh delight. It was about seventy miles off. Its appearance was rugged and spiral, and very similar to a Swiss mountain. Just before reaching camp the travellers encountered some natives of the Masai tribe, with sheep and goats which they had raided from the Wakamba. Their spears were still stained with the blood of those whom they had attacked. The Masai are at present a great source of anxiety and difficulty to the British officials. They do no work, agricultural or otherwise, and they live by raiding the neighbouring tribes. They drive their stolen herds from pasture to pasture, and literally live by murder and rapine. When on the war-path, they seem entirely devoid of feeling, spearing men, women, and children indiscriminately, and often cruelly torturing their victims before putting them to death. The contrast they present to the Wakamba is very marked. These latter are very shy of Europeans, and can hardly be got to come near to trade. The Masai walk straight up and shake hands, obviously thinking themselves quite on a par with any Musungu (European). This tribe, as well as the Wakikuyu, have no respect for human life, nor have they ever even heard the Gospel. Some of them, years back, begged Dr. Baxter to live among them and teach them. But at present, with the exception of the newly started "Central African Mission," which, as has before been noticed, works amongst the Wakamba, there is no missionary effort being made for these three tribes. The country all round Kikuyu is very thickly populated. Many villages and stockades, containing unknown numbers of men and women, are hidden among the beautiful hills and trees. No praise or prayer is offered in "the Name which is above every name," because that Name has never been proclaimed to them. The contrast between the great supply of teachers at home, and the unnumbered thousands of heathen in these regions alone, entire strangers to the news of salvation, with no teacher at all, is heartbreaking to contemplate. May the flag of the late East African Company, with its picture of a sunrise, be indeed a blessed prophecy, and the day be hastened when " the Sun of Righteousness shall arise" upon the darkness of East Africa "with healing in His wings." If this vast country, for which England has made herself responsible, is not to be mocked by a mere godless civilization, Christians in England must see to it at once.

A very interesting account of a visit to a heathen gathering is given in one of our young missionary's circular letters. He went with Dr. Cook, Miss Bird, and Miss Timpson to a kraal, about three-quarters of a mile from the Fort, in which live about 2,000 Wakikuyu with their Chief. The Chief is an intelligent man, who has welcomed English protection for himself and his people. Word had been sent that the missionaries were coming to take sketches, so some of the warriors were outside awaiting them. The Wakikuyu warriors carry long heavy spears, and wear a profusion of beads and brass rings round their necks and arms. The more wealthy of them betoken their superiority by smearing their faces and shoulders with red ochre. The visitors enjoyed a warm reception with hearty hand-shaking. The kraal is quite hidden from view, and contains thatched mud-houses, and is strongly guarded by short stakes. The entrance is through several narrow archways, in height six yards or thereabout, formed of stakes thirty feet long driven into the ground. The Chief's twenty-five wives,

7

mostly with children strapped to their backs, crowded round with much curiosity. The Chief is a man about thirty-five years of age, and decidedly superior to the rest of his tribe. Dr. Cook photographed the Chief with his little son and heir, about six years old, between his knees, while the wives and warriors stood on either side. Some of the houses also were sketched and painted. The children running about were several of them much diseased in their feet and legs, while ophthalmia was common to many, both young and old. It was a striking sight to see Miss Bird speaking to the Chief in Swahili (which he understood) of the love of God in Christ. He sat on the ground with several chiefs around. After singing some Swahili hymns, she told him of the Bwana Isa Masieya (Lord Jesus Christ). He knew the name, probably having heard it at the coast, which he had once visited, and where he learned Swahili. Every now and then he passed on to his chiefs in his own tongue what Miss Bird had told him in Swahili. All listened most attentively. Miss Bird's "boy" is a bright Free Town Christian lad. He had accompanied her in order to carry her chair. She told him to say to the Chief that what she spoke of was for the black as well as the white people. The "boy" did so very simply in Swahili, and the Chief seemed to take in all he said. Afterwards Miss Bird asked if he would like some Christian teachers to come to his people. He replied that he would confer with the elders of the tribe, and bring word when he visited the missionaries' camp on the morrow. The visit duly took place. He brought with him eight of his chiefs, and they expressed their willingness to receive a missionary. The Chief much enjoyed his four cups of tea, as well as biscuits, acid drops, and chocolate. It was most amusing to see the guests sitting round, silently munching the chocolate. The Chief called in at the Fort on his way home, and reported that the English "bibi" (ladies) had filled him well. He was evidently thoroughly satisfied both in mind and body by his reception. Miss Timpson had worked his name on a fez cap, and pinned on a small likeness of the Queen. He was delighted with this, and sat with it on during his visit. He made the party handsome presents of fat sheep on his return. For the first time the Word of Life was thus preached in these parts. The Gospel had never been proclaimed within a radius of at least 200 miles from this spot. The effect of this little visit was to make the preachers more than ever fascinated with the joyous, blessed work to which they had been

called. John adds: " The burden of the thousands
of souls sitting in darkness between the coast and
Uganda must weigh upon the Church at home,
till she gives some of her best sons and daughters
for the sowing and the reaping of these ' fields
white already to harvest.' Teaching and preaching are called for loudly, and we as missionaries
can only supply the need by constant learning and
praying. I do want to be an apostolic missionary,
and give myself continually to prayer and the
ministry of the Word. The opportunities and
calls for work are unbounded. It is impossible at
home to realize what heathenism is—the hopelessness and viciousness and cruelty are so great.
Whatever remnants of doubt there might be as
to whether I did right in coming out here have
some time ago fled."

There was a delay of some days at Kikuyu
owing to transport difficulties. The nights were
very cold. John had to sleep in pants, flannel
trousers, and shirt, pyjama jacket, cholera belt,
and flannel belt under two jaeger blankets, one
rug, and one shawl! During breakfast, just before sunrise, the chilliness was often so keen that
he had to eat his porridge, etc., wrapped up in
shawls. And *this* on the Equator! In the morning the water was like iced water. Still the

climate is most healthy for Englishmen. Kikuyu had been marked out to be the great half-way centre for the railway. But, as it is perched at a height of 6,000 or more feet above the sea, difficulties are anticipated in bringing the line up so high. Possibly the nearest station will be about twenty miles off, and a branch line will be run to Kikuyu. The natives are most unwilling to part with their land for that or any other purpose, and it is exceedingly difficult to induce them to barter and trade. Under the Company, the officials took a very high hand, and walked off with what flocks and goods they needed, not always paying anything in return. The same officials—now under Government—have had to treat the natives with more consideration. The country is being rapidly opened up, and very lately Kikuyu has been put within the Postal Union. John had two attacks of fever while at Kikuyu within three days, but, thanks to the care and treatment of Dr. Baxter, was enabled quickly to throw them off. His "boy," Thomas, too, was most attentive when his "Bwana" was ill. At times it seemed impossible to get warm. Malarial fever makes a man shiver inside and out—through and through. After piling all available blankets on the bed Thomas literally heaped clothes upon the top, and then the shivering changed to perspiration.

Kikuyu was left on the 16th, after a substantial lunch at the Fort, picnic fashion. The party set out along a path made by the Government, and camped, after a 5½ miles march, near a remarkable swamp. It is really a lake in a most beautiful situation. It is covered on the surface with six inches of grass and duckweed. The water is very deep, and clear underneath. The natives have made paths across the surface, which look most unsafe. No Englishman has yet ventured across. It being found that the bullock cart could not carry enough food to allow of a Sunday rest, the travellers had to march on the Sunday. They tramped 17½ miles, enjoying most exquisite mountain views. The first part of the walk was through beautiful English park-like scenery with many flowers. Everything was very green, as there is rain at this time of year almost nightly. The breeze was fresh and invigorating, and quite braced John up after his attacks of fever. At one point in the march they were at a height of 7,400 feet above sea-level. Looking down, they saw mountain rising above mountain, the intervening plain-land studded with trees and rocks, shadowed now and again by passing clouds in the sunshine. Each successive camp seemed more beautiful than the last. The sky in these parts is exquisitely blue and clear. They descended the steep encampment to the lower plain, and found themselves at the site of the attack of Masai on Mr. Dick's caravan in November, 1895, just after the last missionary party had passed that way. Mr. Dick, with two other Europeans, was returning to the coast with a number of porters. The latter interfered with some of the Masai, and opened their cattle kraal, letting out their cows. The Masai protested, but were pushed aside by the porters. One of the Askaris at last fired at a Masai. They then raised their war-cry, and thousands of Masai rushed down the hills upon the caravan. They speared twenty Swahili or Wakikuyu porters, as well as Mr. Dick himself. About eighteen Askaris and the two other Europeans stood in a circle, and kept back the Masai with their rifles ; the porters were, of course, unarmed. A short time after this massacre the late Sir Gerald Portal was met here by some Masai chiefs on his way up country. They declared that they did not wish to fight the Europeans, but were quite prepared to do so if forced. The missionary party reached camp at 2 p.m. on the Sunday afternoon, at the foot of

some mountains covered with trees, and close to
a shallow, bubbling river.   Dr. Baxter did not
come in till 3.30, as he had stayed behind
to struggle with the obstreperous bullocks in the
cart.   They persisted in lying down in the road
with their necks tightly fixed under the yokes.
The Holy Communion was celebrated at 5 in
Mr. Baskerville's tent.   Hymns followed, and a
blessed time of soul refreshment was enjoyed.
At night there was a tremendous wind, and the
tent seemed to be in danger of being blown
away.   John writes : " We had visions of pursu-
ing and stalking our tents in the early morning
across the mountains !   It did not come to this,
owing to the exertions of Dr. Baxter, who seemed
to spend half the night going from tent to tent
fastening down the ropes and pegs."

A short march of 8½ miles on Monday was
followed by a much longer one of 20½ miles on
Tuesday.   They started at 5.45 a.m.   The sunrise upon the mountains was most grand.
They skirted Lake Naivasha for about eight
miles, passing two extinct volcanoes.   The loveliness of the scenery here passed description.
John compares the air to Cromer air, only as ·
more invigorating and less chilling.   The climate
was most bracing and yet warm, and the nights

not so bitterly cold as at Kikuyu. Every day found them on the march, including two Sundays, until they arrived at the Fort in Eldoma Ravine on January 27th. The two Sunday marches were exceptionally long—one of 19 miles, and the other of 22½ miles. Scarcity of porters' food compelled them to press on. Major Smith was in command of the Nubian troops at Naivasha Fort. His love for Africa had caused him to refuse the colonelcy of one of the Guards' regiments which had been offered him. He sent into camp a large quantity of delicious fresh milk, which proved a most welcome change on " Nestlé." Twice only had the party enjoyed bread and butter since leaving the coast. At this time the transport service from the coast was almost at a standstill, so many of the porters being employed on the railway. A few bullock waggons were running; but the first 150 miles from the coast are fatal to cattle owing to the tsetse fly, at least 50 per cent. dying before Kibwezi can be reached. All this difficulty will disappear when once the railway is constructed. The country through which the caravan had been passing lately abounds in game. Dr. Baxter and other sportsmen in the company kept the table well supplied with zebra and antelope flesh.

Soup made from zebra's brain was a luxury, unknown, indeed, in England, but much relished. On Sundays the rule was—"No shooting!" This showed the Swahili porters that the missionaries reverenced the first day of the week. As might be expected, the game seemed to come specially near on the Sundays. On one Sunday in particular two hyænas, some beautifully marked antelopes, and an ostrich, passed close to the caravan. They all seemed to realize that they were safe that day from rifles and bullets. Lions were not so troublesome as formerly, but the Askaris, who were watching the donkeys, reported that two lions gazed very longingly at the steeds one night near to their "boma," but, fearing the camp fires, at last slunk away. Elephants have appeared on the scene, and their marks were visible everywhere. At Naivasha the party found a German explorer and scientist encamped for the night. He had been touring in British East Africa to compare it with the portion of country which had fallen to his own "Fatherland." Before leaving his camp he had strewn the ground with poisoned meat, to destroy some of the many hyænas. The result was that all round the camping ground lay dead hyænas and vultures. One of the ladies lost a little dog, which she had brought from Mombasa. It died in ten minutes. The camp was most unpleasant owing to the number of decaying bodies, which had attracted the " siafu "—the biting ants—which are the scavengers of the country. In the evening Miss Taylor found her tent besieged by " siafu," and the Askaris had to move it. They found her out again and she had to beat a hasty retreat into Miss Timpson's tent. Early next morning they rushed Dr. Baxter's tent. They march along in millions, and, as they bite fiercely, carry all before them. When they take it into their heads to march through a tent, or over a bed, there is nothing for it but for the owner to clear out and leave them in possession. John found several in his pith helmet, and suffered accordingly. The camp was by the side of a large salt lake with beautiful craggy hills on the farther side, and, had it, not been for the nuisance just mentioned, would have been most comfortable.

On Sunday, the 24th, the caravan struck off on the " New Road," which has been made during the last eighteen months between Kikuyu and Lake Victoria. It is a rough road, made for bullock carts, and ascending most of the hills. It is, moreover, very dangerous, as the natives in that part, the Wakamasiya, are rather inclined

to attack European caravans. This people resent
the European appropriation of their country, the
new road passing through their cultivated lands.
They had destroyed a local mail bag about ten
days before, also killing a man and a child. After
leaving Naivasha on the Friday following, just
after the tents were put up, a caravan came from
up country belonging to Mr. Berkeley—the Con-
sul or Commissioner of Uganda. He is successor
to Sir Gerald Portal, and was then on his way
to Europe on furlough. When he came in sight,
Dr. Baxter went to meet him. He turned into
John's tent for tea and biscuits. He was accompanied by Mr. Jackson, in command of the fort
at Eldoma Ravine, the official who gave the first
Company's flag to King Mwanga. That night
the missionary party entertained Mr. Berkeley at
quite a grand dinner in two of the tents placed
end to end. The ladies and the black coolies
were very busy all the afternoon preparing, and
the result was very creditable. The entertainment
was wound up with the National Anthem, sung
standing, at the highly respectable hour of 8.45
p.m. The Baganda porters and boys thought it
a great privilege to have the important Musungu
Chief Bwana Berkeley to dinner. The boys who
waited at table dressed up in their very best,

"which," John remarks, "was wonderful to behold." Mr. Berkeley has done his utmost to
further missionary work in Uganda, and the time
spent with him was very enjoyable.

The next day the caravan dared the perils of
the New Road, and reached the Fort at Eldoma
Ravine in safety. It was necessary to have a
strong guard of Askaris, and to keep them awake
at their posts. They are a sleepy set, and, to
keep one another awake, they shout Arabic
numbers every few minutes. Still they have to
be overlooked and watched, lest somnolency
should prevail. The Fort is on a hill about 400
feet high, and the tents were pitched close by,
about 150 feet lower. The Wakamasiya mentioned above looked a fine set of men. They had
plenty of paint on their bodies, and were armed
with spears and shields all ready for action.
John notes it as a remarkable thing that the
tribal name with one of its syllables omitted is
the Swahili name for "Christian." "Wakama-
sieya" = "people of Masieya (Christ)." There are
no Christian Missions among them, and they have
never heard of the Saviour. He adds : "May
the Wamasiya soon become Wamasieya! They
will then no longer wish to spear and shoot with
arrows those who are brethren ! Will those at

home remember the tribe—just one more among
the many we pass who sit in darkness and the
shadow of death?" Interesting details follow of
a Government Road party of about 500 men,
which was encountered returning from Port
Victoria on the Victoria Nyanza. It consisted
mostly of Indians, with about 400 head of cattle,
and neat iron bullock waggons. There were in
the caravan a number of Beloochees, who had
come over from Kurrachee. The next caravan
met with was one made up of Arabs, Swahilis,
and "Bluchers," with 2,000 donkeys. They had
been up into Abyssinia to buy ivory, and were
now returning to the coast after three years'
absence. Here was a chance not to be despised!
Dr. Baxter bought thirty donkeys to replace
those disabled or dead. The ladies bought a
donkey each for their own use in Uganda, and
Mr. Baskerville bought three. They are most
useful on itinerating work. Several little donkeys
were born on our Safari, and trotted along gamely
when but a few hours old. It is not, perhaps,
wonderful that only one survived.

The Eldoma Ravine is very famous. But a
visit to it is attended with some risk, as the
Wamasiya lurk amongst the trees and hills to
shoot at stray travellers. However, the three

ladies and two other members of the party
(including John) were escorted to the Ravine by
Dr. Macpherson, who is stationed at the fort with
a guard of half a dozen Soudanese troops (probably once part of Emin Pasha's army). There
are to be seen a fine waterfall with a descent
of more than 100 feet, fresh green trees, ferns
clothing all the bottom of the Ravine, which goes
down from 300 to 400 feet, and has a width of
650 feet. Altogether it is a very romantic spot.

A graphic description follows of the manner
and order of the daily march. The horn is blown
at 5. A few minutes later the caravan drum is
beaten by one of the Askaris. Half an hour
after that it is beaten again as a signal for the
taking down of the tents—the boxes, beds, etc.,
having to be packed up during the interval.
Breakfast is partaken of in the open air, and the
plates, spoons, etc., as soon as done with, pounced
upon by the " boys," who are anxious to set off
before the heat succeeds the coldness. The sun
is then beginning to throw ever-brightening tints
on the mountains. The air is often like that
of a frosty English morning. There is time and
opportunity for a quiet reading of the morning
psalms alone. And then comes the start all
together. The new camp is reached at different

times in the morning or afternoon, according to
circumstances. Biscuits and potted meat are
carried for lunch, with water bottles. The " tent "
loads always leave camp first, so as to be in the
new camp as early as possible. The tents are
put up about half an hour after arrival. The
caravan proper, headed by the drum, is often
nearly an hour later. Then, after a little delay,
comes change of garments, and a cold bath, where
the quantity and quality of the water render it
possible. After lunch, which is necessarily a
movable feast, follows reading and a special
study of Luganda. A Muganda Christian porter
named Eriya used to come to John's tent every
afternoon, and they read St. Matthew's Gospel
together. John writes of him : " I don't know
whether I help him much, but he certainly does
my own soul good. His earnest, thoughtful face,
as we read together the Word of Life, speaks
more plainly than any words of his love for it.
He is far too good for a porter. . . . I should
much like to have him as a catechist when we
reach Uganda. He has a wife in Mengo, who,
with him, was instructed by Mr. Millar and Mr.
Roscoe. They were both baptized together. The
joy of being able to speak a little to these men
is very great. It is a real anticipation of the joy

awaiting us in the work when we can speak more fluently.

When there happens to be a day off, the missionary's occupations are manifold. Button-sewing, blanket-stitching, jinricksha-mending, test his skill as an all-round man, and he generally comes off successfully.

Four days' march, in which a distance of fifty-five miles was covered, brought the caravan to Fort Nandi, fifty miles from Lake Victoria Nyanza. It arrived there on Sunday, the 31st January, escorted by Captain Bagnall with his Nubian troops. The march was terribly uphill, the camp having to be pitched at an altitude of 9,500 feet in one place. The way led through several thick forests, composed of a variety of beautiful trees, some of them 200 feet in height. Bamboo trees were common. They grow very tall, and are most graceful. The porters were glad of the opportunity to replenish their supply of tent-poles, which they cut from the bamboos. African forts are generally very unsubstantial erections. They consist of an enclosure surrounded by loose stones or wooden stakes. The entrances are two or three drawbridges of a rough pattern, guarded by sentries, who salute every European in a rough-and-ready fashion. Below the wall of defence

8

outside is a steep trench, and any natives attempt-
ing to scale the wall would be easily shot down
whilst in the trench.   All round, beyond the
trench, is a line of barbed wire.   Inside the enclosure are a number of huts, where the garrison
live with their wives.   The Nubian soldiers have
at least six wives apiece, who work for them,
and carry their tents and goods on the march.
Each man makes his own private mark with a
knife upon his wives' cheeks and arms.   The scars
thus caused do not add to their beauty.   They
carry their infants—native fashion—strapped to the
back, in addition to the load upon the head.   Floating
over each fort is the " Union Jack," claiming the
country for England.   John remarks here, " May
the Church of Christ soon claim the souls of its
inhabitants for Him! The men and women will
then look on one another as heirs together of the
grace of eternal life!   What a glorious change ! "

The   Wa-nandi   tribe — now   reached — have
neither Mission station nor Christian teacher
amongst them.   They are a fine race of men,
and have their own marked distinction in appearance and language from other tribes.   A crowd
assembled round the missionary party when they
were having their first meal.   John offered one of
the spear-armed warriors a few crumbs of cabinet

biscuits. He took them readily, examined very carefully the Musungu's food, but was afraid to eat any. Mr. Clayton gave a girl a potted meat pie with a few pieces of meat. She put some in her mouth, but her father, who was near, would not allow her to swallow it. The Wa-nandi think the food is charmed, and that it will poison them. In Africa every one's hand is against his fellow, and so every one is suspicious of every one else.

An English service was held in two tents placed together at 5 p.m., at which John officiated as chaplain, speaking from 2 Corinthians iv. 5. (This address is particularly referred to in letters of Dr. Cook and Mr. Clayton after his home-call.) There was a specially sweet realization of the Divine Presence, and much fervour in prayer. Amongst the congregation were Mr. Bagge, the civilian in charge of the Fort, and a young American, who was on his way to Mengo to take charge of some stores, which were to be opened there by Messrs. Smith and Mackenzie of Mombasa. The opportunities which the Europeans at the various forts have of attending public worship are so few, and their influence for good or ill is so great, that the responsibility of "speaking in the Name of Jesus" in their presence is no slight one.[1]

[1] See testimony as to this sermon in two letters.

After the evening meal Mr. Baskerville and Dr.
Baxter held services, as usual, for the Swahili and
Baganda in the caravan, and the next day, at
7.30, seven of the missionaries enjoyed blessed
and refreshing fellowship with one another and
the Lord at His table.

The next day, and the day following, marches
of above twelve miles were accomplished down
towards the lake, in the shade of thick leafy
forests, under a warmer atmosphere. John had
the great pleasure here of meeting for a few
minutes a Plumstead friend—Mr. McAllister, the
son of the Vicar of St. Nicolas, Plumstead. He
is connected with the Government in the Uganda
Protectorate, and was then on his way to the
coast. But a greater pleasure still was in store—
the arrival of the mail with long-expected letters
from home. Let us describe the scene in John's
own words. "What a rush there was for letters!
There were, besides Government bags, twelve
C.M.S. bags containing letters, papers and parcels.
The way-bills were eagerly searched, and most
of the sacking of these bags was ripped up, as
our letters were some in one bag, some in another.
These were our first letters from home since about
November 25th. A large bath was brought out,
and all letters belonging to our party were hastily

thrown in, as they were discovered in the various bags. A good bath-load was the result of the searching. Then each fished out his or her own property, and during the rest of the day the camp was absolutely quiet, so far as the Europeans were concerned. It is impossible to answer all the pile of most welcome letters from warm-hearted friends by this mail, which goes away to-morrow. I will answer them individually (all well) by the mail which reaches England about the end of May. Fresh news is among the "all things" which a missionary to Central Africa and his friends have to give up. I think, if friends in England could have seen our delight in getting letters, they would have felt well repaid for their labour of love in writing." John received at this time the welcome intelligence of the birth of a nephew at Walton, and sent special congratulations to its "grandparents."

The next two days the heat proved excessive, and the caravan was compelled to halt before 11 o'clock. They passed out of the country of the Wa-nandi into that of the Wa-kavirondo on the north-east of the Victoria Nyanza. These latter are quite a different people, both in customs and appearance, from any hitherto encountered. Their houses are neater than those of any other. They

swarmed into the camp as soon as the tents were
pitched, bringing sheep, honey, eggs, bananas, etc.,
etc., for sale.   The exchange was made with chains
of beads and copper-wire brought from the coast.
It is very amusing to note the different fashions
as to beads in the various districts.   At one place
they must be pink and large ; at another, red, and
square.   The Wa-kavirondos' ideas of "dress" are
limited to the wearing of a few strings of beads
round the neck.   A clergyman in England some
time ago offered to support two missionaries to
work amongst this people.   Up to the present
time the men, alas ! have not been forthcoming,
and this tribe, like all the rest, is in complete
ignorance of God's way of salvation.

Chapter VII

"Ethiopia shall soon stretch out her hands unto God."—
Ps. lxviii. 31.

A T length, on Monday, February 15th, after over eleven weeks' tramp, Mengo was reached by those of the party who crossed the Victoria Nyanza from Kavirondo. The voyage was most interesting. It commenced at midday on Thursday, the 11th, in the small steam launch *Ruwenzori*, the joint property of the C.M.S. and Messrs. Boustead & Ridley, of Mombasa. The travellers had to sleep on board that night, the ladies packed into the small cabin, and the six men sleeping on the cabin roof, "lying," as John says, "like a layer of sardines." The Lake was most beautiful, with several islands in sight in the moonlight. Next day, there being no coal in those ports, and firewood running short, they went ashore in Pringle Bay to replenish their stores.

Here they stayed all the next day while the natives cut down wood. These were Wasoga (the people of Busoga), and very hospitable, although they have the reputation of being great thieves. The party breakfasted and pitched their tents among lovely banana groves. In a village close by they found some "lubare" huts outside the native dwellings. These are built as habitations for spirits, and resemble tiny native huts. On the Saturday the camp was pitched on the island of Ugaza. The people were very much alarmed, breaking up their market when the steamer approached. Most of them fled over the hills or in their canoes. Those who remained were friendly, and, in the evening, some native Christians came to the ladies, asking them to read and pray. These had been instructed and baptized at Mengo, and had returned about three weeks before to teach their fellow-islanders. They begged hard for books, having only one Testament among them. But this need could not then be supplied. A start forward had to be made the next day (Sunday, February 7th), as there was again a difficulty about firewood and food supply. That afternoon a descent was made on the mainland, and the missionary party stood for the first time on the soil of Uganda. In the evening a service was held ; Mr. Clayton read the Church Prayers, and hymns followed outside the ladies' tent. There were only three tents between nine people. On Monday, for the last time, they embarked on the *Ruwenzori*. Leaving Port Alice away to the west, they steamed almost due north to Munyonya, the nearest landing-place to Mengo, where they arrived at noon. For the last time they dropped themselves and their luggage into the native canoes which came alongside. For the last time they clung to the backs of stalwart natives, who waded with them through swampy mud and reeds, landing them within seven miles of the capital. A messenger was sent forward to announce their arrival. Meanwhile, with hearts full of gratitude to God for journeying mercies, under spreading palm and banana trees, they sang the Doxology, and John read part of the Consecration Prayer in the Communion Office aloud, all joining in the Lord's Prayer.

After making the necessary arrangements in regard to their luggage they began their walk. The time of their arrival was not known, or they would have been met. The first person to greet them when they had got on about two miles was Mr. Leakey, of Koki, whom John well remembered as an undergraduate at Corpus Christi College,

Cambridge. He came running, bathed in perspiration, having made all haste forward as soon
as the messenger arrived. He reported that the
ladies were not far behind. What followed shall
be given in John's own words : " By this time
men and boys, with long, spotless, white robes,
ran to and from us, bringing us greetings, and
running back to tell the Mengo missionaries. The
Uganda salutation is unique. The men and boys
stoop, and, placing their hands on their knees, say
' Otyano ? ' (how are you, sir ?). The answer to
this is a grunt, 'Aye,' to which the one first
addressed says, ' Aye.' After this you tell them
that you are 'bulungi' (quite well). The polite
inquirer then asks, ' Agapayo ? ' (how are things at
home ?). You then assure him they too are
' mungi ' (in a satisfactory condition). You are
then expected to inquire after the Muganda health
and domestic affairs. The particular salutations
of the different tribes on the way were very
interesting. The Swahili say ' Yambo ' (a word
with you). The Masai say ' Horo,' the meaning
of which is uncertain. The Wa-kavirondos' is the
best. They greet a stranger with ' Emirembe '
(peace). Grunts form a great part of the Luganda
salutation, and the right intonations are most
important. But to return to our walk to Mengo.

Three of the Mission ladies met us, and rushed into
the arms of the three who had come with us.
Women belonging to the Church were with them,
and greeted the new ladies most affectionately.
Next we met the Archdeacon (the Ven. R. H.
Walker), the Rev. A. J. Pike, and another lady.
We were now nearing the hill from which the
church at the top had been seen for some time.
The hill Namerembi is all church property ; it is
covered with banana trees, among which the missionaries' houses are built. We met Miss Furley
here near to the King's Compound. The Katikiro
(prime minister) lives opposite the king's big entrance. He is a Christian, and most regular at
church. Hearing of our arrival, he came to his
gate and welcomed us warmly. The Katikiro is a
fine man in every sense of the word. He has actually more power than Mwanga, the king. Our
appearance in the fine roads had attracted much
attention ; men, women, and children pressing
round to clasp our hands. As may be imagined,
the Uganda salutation, even when somewhat cur-
tailed, causes no small delay when rehearsed again
and again. 'Had we had a good journey?' 'We
rejoice to see you :' these and such-like greetings
abounded. The warm-heartedness of this truly
wonderful people has not been at all exaggerated.

We felt at home at once. Among the crowd were
Mohammedans, who looked on indifferently, while
Roman Catholic Christians also mostly held aloof.
Some of the latter however shook hands cordially.
Dr. Baxter, Mr. Clayton and I were sheltered and
fed that night at the house of the Rev. E. Millar,
Dr. Baxter sleeping on his dining-room table!
The houses are built of reeds. They are mostly
cool, but only last about three years, if they
escape being burnt down sooner. Fires often
occur, chiefly through the custom of making wood
fire on the floors, the smoke ascending to the lofty
arched roof without any chimney. . . .

"On waking at 5.30 we heard drums being
beaten in the compound of the Christian chiefs, as
the men and boys live at some distance from one
another. The chiefs summon them thus to
Family Prayers morning by morning. Classes
are held in the buildings round, and in the
church itself, from 8 to 9 a.m. At 9 one of the
native clergy takes the service. The daily morning service is wonderful. The church is quite half
full with a congregation of men, women, and
growing children. The Katikiro sits on a chair
in the front with his children at his feet. All the
rest sit, as is usual with natives, on the floor.
Most bring mats—also their Testaments and

ROOM IN REV. ERNEST MILLAR'S HOUSE, MENGO, UGANDA

hymn books, and the rustle of turning over leaves is very marked. One of the ladies leads the singing on a small portable harmonium—an instrument quite inadequate. Mr. Wilson has ordered a £60 organ as a gift to his church, and it is now on its way.

" The first afternoon several of us went to see the king with Mr. Millar and Mr. Leakey. Many courtyards, containing loungers and hangers-on, were passed through before we came to the waiting-house close to the palace. We were not kept waiting long, and entered the palace—a well-built, two-storied house, with a staircase (the only one I have seen). Ascending this, we were ushered into the royal presence, after being warned not to tread on the king's carpet. Mwanga is better looking than most of his pictures make him, and is a shrewd fellow. He rose, and received us courteously. We shook hands in European fashion, and then sat on the stools which attendants brought in. The king sat on the floor, with a courtier by his side facing him, whose attentions and fawnings disgusted us. Mwanga asked our names, and tried to learn them. He then asked if we had seen the Queen in England; also, how old she was. Hearing that she was nearly eighty, he was much surprised.

Africans rarely live to anything approaching this
age. His next question was, 'Have you any
coats or waistcoats to sell?' Mr. Whitehouse
replied that he had a waistcoat to spare, and the
next afternoon Mwanga sent for it. Mr. Millar
and Mr. Leakey talked and laughed with the
king, and, when anything was said which made
the king laugh, the courtier at once laughed too.
The latter watched the king's every movement,
the king, when amused, holding out his hand,
which the courtier pressed with both his own.
Mwanga sang us a song, accompanying it himself with his native lyre. We soon afterwards
took leave."

On the day of his arrival at Mengo, John received his appointment to Toro—a huge district
5,000 square miles or so in extent, 200 miles
from Mengo, "a region of snow mountains and
pigmies" (as he calls it), almost in the very heart
of Africa, the most distant Mission from the East
Coast. It has been worked since last May by
Mr. Fisher and Mr. Lloyd, the former of whom is
returning to England on furlough. It forms part
of the Uganda general Protectorate, and there
are, therefore, resident European officers. The
language is not Luganda, though akin to it, but
the teaching is done in Luganda, as there are no

printed books in the vernacular. John remarks : " This is the post to which the senior missionaries here appoint me. After all the prayer offered for their guidance, it must be the Divine Will, and I ask most earnestly the prayers and praises of all who read this circular letter. It was never my wish to be a country parson, but I am going to be one on a rather large scale." The name of the King of Toro is Kasagama, and the country is called " Kasagama's," and is situated at the foot of the Ruwenzori Mountain. The king was baptized in Mengo last March, after instruction by Baganda teachers. The next two or three days were taken up mainly by preparations for the journey. As no provisions could be obtained on the way to Toro it was necessary to lay in a good supply.

On Sunday, February 22nd, the usual service was held in the cathedral church at Mengo at 8. There must have been nearly a thousand people present. Mr. Baskerville preached the sermon. The service was finished by 11. About 300 native Christians received the Holy Communion. There was a second service at 3, when the Rev. H. R. Sugden (a visitor) preached.

The Church Council, in which the native church members are much interested, is held twice a week

in the vestry under the presidency of the Rev. H.
Wright Duta, with all the European missionaries
as friendly assessors. Many most serious offences
committed by communicants have to be dealt
with. When a native Christian becomes slack in
the Christian race, he falls down to even below the
heathen standard of morality, if such a standard
exists at all. The results are most deplorable.
Mengo needs much the prayers as well as the
praises of the Church at home.

On Monday an expedition was made to visit
Mtesa's tomb, part of which was built by
Alexander Mackay. It forms a kind of native
thatched mausoleum, and several heathen attendants are always present. Mr. Leakey ventured to take up one of the spear-heads which
surround it, but the attendants remonstrated,
fearing that the spirit, in whose honour they were
placed there, would resent it. Mtesa is known
among the Baganda to-day as the Mukaba, "the
man who made the people cry." The capital of
Uganda seems to have been moved from one to
another of the many hills at the decease of each
king. A visit was next paid to Mtesa's sister, a
Christian woman, who lives near her brother's
burial-place. Several people were visiting her,
as she was ill, and two dear little princesses about

eight years old ran out to meet us. The royal lady was lying on her couch, troubled with a cough, surrounded by sympathetic friends. The party were warmly welcomed, and she displayed much interest in hearing of the different parts of the country to which they were going. On the walls hung several Luganda texts and a C.M.S. almanack for 1897. A visit just at this time to Archdeacon Walker was most helpful to our young missionary. He was able to tell him a great deal about Toro, and, as the archdeacon knew Norwich well, it was pleasant and cheering to talk over Norwich and friends there. Only that morning, when reading of the sheep gate in St. John's Gospel, Mika Sematimba had mentioned the sheep market on Norwich hill. He had been much struck, when visiting that city, with the sheep in their pens in the market.

About this time John writes to Miss Durnford : " May I beg your constant and fervent prayer for me and the Lord's work in Toro? Please ask others for the same. At present there is no sign of anything like the awakening which has taken place in Mengo and Uganda. But 'God is able,' and the prayers of you and others will be abundantly answered. Hearts will be opened by the Holy Ghost. We shall be ' workers together

9

with ' one another and with Him. Missionary news will not, I expect, be of an *exciting* kind for some time at least. It will be a time of patient sowing the seed in faith. It seems quite the proper thing to say that there is no comparison between the needs of England and heathen countries. The sins—many too awful to speak of— and the ignorance of the people appal any Christian after the comparatively high public opinion of even worldly people in England. There is hopelessness and mere existence, with no love or true joy, everywhere. The faces of the old people are so sad ; they speak of blank and blighted souls, without a ray of light to brighten the valley of death. They know of no living Christ. Everything is *very real*; the fight against the Evil One is no mere figure of speech. But it is blessed to remember that out of '*every* tribe ' *some* at least shall sing the new song in the presence of the Lamb . . . I long for God—more of Himself. In communion with Him, though separated in body, all in Christ meet. This is the chief joy for me and her who has beén given me in the Lord. We are so near to Him, and He will bring us together ' for Him ' in His time, to fight together in His power."

Chapter VIII

JOURNEY TO TORO

"As they ministered to the Lord, and fasted, the Holy Ghost said, Separate me Barnabas and Saul for the work whereunto I have called them."—*Acts* xiii. 2.

W E must now accompany our young missionary on the last stage of his journeyings. A great deal that happened will be best told in his own words. The isolation in which he would henceforth have to live seemed to weigh a little on his mind. But he bore up bravely and trustingly, as one who was going in God's strength and under His guidance, to "the very front of the fight." All (he felt) must be well. The difficulties in regard to the language added to his anxiety, Luganda not being the language of the people of Toro. He left Mengo, after a stay of eight days, with the Revs. H. K. Sugden and B. E. Wigram, on Wednesday, February 24th. Before starting he had the pleasure of meeting Mr. Fisher, one of the Toro lay missionaries, on his way to England on furlough. Mr. Fisher had been greatly

blessed during his five years' stay in Africa.
and had opened up work in four new stations,
The pleasure was mutual, for Mr. Fisher writes
subsequently to John's father : "We are all so
thankful that your dear son has been sent to Toro.
He is so strong, and in every way fitted for the
most advanced and difficult Mission in Uganda."
He speaks feelingly of the fellowship they enjoyed during the two days they were together in
Mengo.   He found him full of thankfulness and
hope. "God is going to do the work," he said.
He saw in him a deeply spiritual man—one who
lived near to his Lord and recognised God in
everything, full of love for the natives, who quickly
gathered round him. Four of Mr. Fisher's little
boys who had just arrived with him from Toro
at once decided to go back with John as his
personal boys. Mr. Fisher writes : "He was most
good-natured and thoughtful and kind—qualities
which at once carry a man into the hearts of the
Baganda. One night I was looking for my boy
who was supposed to mind the house, and eventu-
ally found him covered with Mr. Callis's blanket.
He had got fever during my absence, and Callis,
without knowing who he was, covered him up,
and had Dr. Cook to come and see him. We
spoke about shooting, and I remember he said,

'We will not mind a rifle, as there will be no time for shooting.' He was most cheerful and bright. The morning he left Mengo for Toro I walked out with him, chatting about the work, and then came the good-bye and last hand-wave from the top of the hill. Mr. Lloyd has since told me of the conversion of a terrible drunkard in Toro, who was spoken to by Mr. Callis just before his death." The first stage of John's journey to Toro was completed when he reached Mityana, about forty-five miles from Mengo, where Mr. Sugden had been labouring. This took three days. On the way they stopped each night at places where there were churches and native Baganda teachers. Caravan travelling in the country of Buganda was found to be very different from what it had been on the route from the coast. The chiefs of the villages entertained them, providing them with boiled *matoke* (bananas) for themselves and their porters. The porters slept in native houses, and no longer carried tents. There were always several empty and (more or less) clean houses for guests in each village. The people were most hospitable, bringing the Europeans presents of fowls, milk, eating berries, eggs, and sometimes cooked food. Every afternoon, on the move from Mengo to Mityana, Mr. Sugden held short services in the churches. The church drum was beaten, and a congregation of from twenty to fifty earnest worshippers attended. John writes : " To see these native brethren and sisters, with their faces in their hands, bowed to the ground, and to hear their responses and singing, is very beautiful. The Baganda teachers sent to live and preach in the larger villages are a fine body of young men. Their square shoulders, fine physique, and clean, white flowing robes, with their warm, affectionate nature, make them very lovable. They are doing much good work in the countries all round Buganda, as well as in Buganda itself. They are all trained in Mengo. While instructing the country people in the Way of Life, they are themselves most anxious to know more of the truth. They teach the people to read, and instruct them for baptism. One of the European clergy in whose district they work supervises them, visiting the villages in turn, examining and baptizing the candidates for baptism. I have been very much struck with these young Baganda teachers ; they seem full of love and humility."

Mityana was reached on the Friday afternoon, the chiefs and people coming out to welcome Mr. Sugden back from his visit to Mengo. When he told them that he had brought two guests

and that one of them (Mr. Wigram) was going
to stay and live with them, they swung their
heads to and fro, saying, "Neyanza." This is
the Muganda's way of expressing joy and gratitude. John writes again : " It is hard to give any
idea of the warm welcome we receive on all sides.
Africa's hearts are warm, like its climate. The
Mission station and church at Mityana are on a
high hill, the houses being hid away among the
banana plantations. A lake lies to the west, and
the sunsets across the water are very lovely. On
Sunday, at the morning service, I had the very
great joy of taking a very small part in the service.
It consisted only of saying the words in Luganda
for administering the cup in the Holy Communion Service. It was, however, the first time
I had worn my surplice in a Luganda service,
and it was a great joy to minister to the people
even in such a small way. A layman—Mr.
Fletcher—had come to greet us beyond Mityana.
He works under Mr. Sugden at a Mission station
seven hours' walk from there. We had a most
happy Sunday, and it was a hitherto unheard-of
event that four Europeans should be together at
Mityana."

The next morning, cheered and refreshed by
this fellowship in the Lord, John set out on his

lonely journey to Toro. Twenty Batoro porters
carried his baggage. Mr. Fletcher accompanied
him for about a mile, and then he was left, for
the first time since being away from home, without a single fellow European. The porters only
understood Luganda very slightly. Besides them
he had with him his three Baganda "boys," and
one of the Toro teachers, with his wife and small
son of about seven. This Baganda teacher, Isaac,
had been to Mengo for a visit, and was now
returning. He proved most useful in arranging
for the porters at the different camps. A great
feature of the country now entered upon is the
swamp, covered with papyrus plants. Many of
these swamps have had native bridges built across
them by the chiefs. The day John and his party
left Mityana, after marching two hours, they came
to a large swamp, which was really an arm of the
Lake. There was nothing for it but to strip to
the waist and wade it. The mud and water came
up to the waist, and they were one hour and ten
minutes crossing. A sort of road, five or six feet
in width, had been made through the swamp by
cutting down the papyrus plants. On either side
were the other tall plants towering aloft, and,
underneath the surface, innumerable roots. These
latter had an unpleasant habit of catching the

feet as in a snare. In consequence the traveller
would now and again find himself on hands and
feet, floundering in mud and dirty water. The
above was the largest swamp of all, but several
smaller ones had to be crossed in the valleys
between the hills. And this was the mode of
crossing. Elevated on the shoulders of his
" boy " Thomas, with his knees on each side of
Thomas's face, his hands pressing his woolly pate,
and his feet dug closely into his ribs, John was
carried over, in momentary fear and trembling
lest his patient beast of burden should stumble,
and pitch him head first from a height of seven
feet into the slush and mire.

That first afternoon, when the camp had been
pitched, there was a service in church, and John
gave his first address in church in Luganda ; and
at all the places where there was a Protestant
church he held a little informal service to welcome the teachers and people. These churches
are built of reeds, strung closely together ; the
floors are hardened mud, and there is generally
a " reading desk," also built of reeds, with a raised
platform of hardened mud. The service consisted of hymns, reading, and prayer, led by Isaac
and the local Baganda teachers, and a few words
from John, expressing the joy he felt at coming

to the people to teach and preach to them in their own country. One morning the local teacher brought his Luganda Testament, and asked the meaning of the text in which it is said that Christ should "bring forth judgment unto victory." Each day, as the party went on, the Christians brought them on their way, and, on separating to return, said, " Kabonda akukuma " (may God protect you). One day they passed two swarms of locusts. The trees were covered, and the air seemed full of them. The appearance at a distance was that of a snowstorm.

On the third day (Ash Wednesday) after leaving Mityana the camp was pitched for the first time in Roman Catholic territory. The west side of Baganda has no C.M.S. stations, as the chiefs are Romanists. Some caravans of Protestant missionaries have been refused food at Roman Catholic villages. It was, however, on this occasion willingly given. At several places the chiefs at first seemed rather cold and shy, but they have been told to treat the Protestants with suspicion. Ten days were spent in Roman Catholic territory. The people, as a rule, seemed earnest, but ill-instructed Christians. There was the same longing for knowledge of the truth found as amongst the Protestants. They knew enough of the things of Christ to make them long to know more. John writes: "I had delightful times at each village. Sometimes it was sitting on the floor by a chief's side speaking with him and his people, who sit in crowds round the doorway. At other times in the native huts there were always those willing to listen, and to warmly greet one. The Baganda women are great smokers, and they would "thoughtfully sit and smoke while I took a crucifix from a man's neck, and told them of Him who was slain and now reigns. At one place I found Isaac hotly arguing with the chief about the 'Papa.' I had told him something of the claims which the Bishop of Rome makes upon all Christians only the day before. He seized the first opportunity to let it off in arguing with this chief. I went and took the chief's hand, and said, 'Let us talk not of the Pope, but of Christ. He alone is the Saviour.' The dear fellow quite brightened up, and, turning from Isaac, listened most attentively."

The following Sunday was a most happy day. The party arrived on Saturday, hot and tired, after six hours' march, at the chief's enclosure in the large village of Kawanga. The chief (Bisigolo) was gone to read with his Roman Catholic teachers some days' march away, but he was expected back on Sunday morning. The *musigori*, or "steward," had been left in charge, and, upon being applied to, willingly gave the party permission to stay for two days. He was very ill with dropsy. John paid him what he calls "a delightful pastoral visit" in the afternoon, and they parted great friends. On the Sunday a service was held. The porters sat on the ground in the shade of the high courtyard reed wall. John gave out the hymns, and said a little about the words. As they could only understand Luganda when very distinctly spoken, Isaac preached. He took as his text St. John iii. 16 and vii. 37. While the last hymn was being sung, the beating of a drum announced the return home of Bisigolo, the chief, who shortly entered the courtyard with another chief from Budu, a Protestant Christian named Mark. Many of his retainers were with him, carrying his chair and guns. He seemed delighted to find hymns being sung in his courtyard, and greeted all most kindly. Another little service was held in the afternoon—this time outside the courtyard, as the shadow was now in that quarter. John writes: "It was a very enjoyable time, and I wish I could describe it to you. About twenty rough Batoro sat on the ground before me ; on the right of my chair Isaac was

sitting, and, on his right, the Budu chief had the
little folding-up stool. We sang several hymns,
which Mr. Ashe and Mr. Pilkington have translated, such as 'Jesus loves me, this I know';
'Here we suffer grief and pain'; 'Jesus lives!
no longer now.' We sang the choruses again and
again ; it is good to see the hungry look on the
faces of these heathen. Little by little a spiritual
truth seems to dawn upon them. IT IS true that
Africa is waiting ; there is a real stretching out
of the hands unto God. The Budu chief Mako
(Mark) spoke, and he, too, had chosen St. John
iii. 16 as his text, quite unaware that Isaac had
taken it in the morning. It was a sight to do
one's soul good, as the rough country porters
leaned forward, so as not to lose a word which
fell from the chief's lips. We sat just outside
the tall reed entrance to the courtyard, and the
country round, with its hills and trees, was bathed
in sunshine. After the service I went to the house
where Isaac was staying, to see his wife, who was
ill with fever; then to the house of the musigori,
who was still lying under the bananas—the chief,
with several of his attendants, visiting him to tell
of his journey. Bisigolo made room for me on
his mat, and we sat and talked of the things of
God. I read and sang 'While shepherds watched

their flocks by night.' He promised to visit
me in my tent, which he did that evening
when we had a good time together again. He
begged very hard for a New Testament, and
I wrote a note to Mr. Sugden at Mityana for
one of his men to take. If Mr. Sugden had no
books for sale, he said he should send his man
to Mengo, to buy some Testaments for himself
and his people. This Sunday ended with singing
more hymns with the porters in the moonlight
round the camp fire."

The next day a start was made before day-
break, and the midday halt took place on a
hill where there was a large potato field in
charge of one labouring man (Makopi). No
further progress could be attempted that day,
for Isaac and his sick wife were far behind, and
the porters could not be prevailed upon to go
on. The following day's march was, therefore,
a very long and tiring one. At length, a stop
was decided upon at an empty house standing
in the midst of another potato field. Potatoes
were dug up and roasted, and all the trials of
the long march were forgotten. John remarks :
" This seems like taking a great liberty with
other people's property, according to English
ideas ! " From the top of a very high eminence

a splendid view was enjoyed. The hills were topped with cairns of massive grey rock. For miles and miles hill after hill rose all around, and there was hardly any sign of man or village. The pure fresh air was most invigorating. The desolation that was to be seen on every side is due to the slave trade and inter-tribal warfare. That evening John and Isaac turned off the road to visit a place where they had intended to spend the previous night. It consisted of only ten houses, but it was of special interest as being the last village on the east side of the Toro Mission district. John writes: " The chief was a most striking young fellow of about eighteen. He and his mother were most refined ; their lips were thin, and their features very good. They seemed more like Europeans, and quite different from the people they rule. The chief is very slowly learning to read, and I asked him to come and stay with me in Toro. I was delighted with this bright, fine-looking fellow. Many people at home think Africans are a race of heavy, thick-headed, unintelligent people, but little removed from the lower animals. In this part of Central Africa, at any rate, this is perfectly false ; the races are intelligent, and longing for more knowledge."

The camp was pitched that night at Kitagwato, a large Protestant village. John writes: "About two miles off two Baganda teachers ran out to meet me. They carried me over two swamps and some way up the next hill. The chief, Nyama, clothed in a large terai hat and his best clothes, was most hearty in his welcome. He brought me a large pot of a native drink called *mubise*, which was very refreshing. We then went to the church, many people answering the invitation of the church drum. We sang hymns and had prayer, and I told the people how glad I was to be with them. This was my first entrance into 'my parish,' and nothing could exceed the kindness and interest of these people. The greetings I have got here have far more than made up for the past six months of travel."

The next day the porters were unwilling to march for more than two hours. The Batoro porters are much weaker than the Swahili or Baganda men. They easily knock up, and are unable to carry the full 60 lb. load. The following morning John and his "boys" started at 6.15 a.m. for Butiti — a large Christian village, twenty miles from Kasagama's—the capital of Mwenge, a district lying between Toro and

DAVID KASAGAMA, KING OF TORO

Bunyoro. Bishop Tucker had stayed there in the previous summer, and had baptized the king and several of his people. There a most enthusiastic welcome awaited him. The king came to see him in the morning. In the afternoon the church drum was beaten, and a goodly company gathered. All sat facing the end of the church, and seemed thoroughly to enjoy the service. On returning from church John found the king and his " ladies " sitting in the European Mission House. He made some tea, and brought out cabinet biscuits and a few dates (remnants of luxuries brought from the coast). The king's wife broke up the hard biscuits, and handed pieces all round to her attendant ladies. They appreciated the biscuits immensely, thinking it a great treat to have some food from Ebulaya (England). At sunset John returned the king's visit, and thus describes the interview : " I found him a most quiet, thoughtful Christian. He said he had many villages, and his people were many. Was I strong ? Had I strength to walk to these people? When I told him that this was the very thing I had come to do, he said quite pathetically, ' They worship lubare, because they do not know God.' Lubare is the name of the heathen deity of these parts. While I was

10

with the king a drum was beaten, and his household assembled for evening prayer. In the dark they sang two hymns from memory, and then the king led his people in prayer. It was a sight which made me feel what a privilege it was to be sent to this place. The king was most generous in his gifts, and sent me a goat, milk, eating bananas, and cooked food for both midday and evening meals. It should be mentioned that the king has built a house for the missionaries to use whenever they come to visit him and his people. He is also building a large new church, as the present one is old and too small for the increasing attendance." On the way to pay this visit to the king John called on the Majessa — the biggest chief. He was sitting in his garden with many followers, and nursing his small baby, which was covered with sores. The baby was brought round in the evening, and John rubbed on some vaseline and bound its arms and legs.

There were eight readers anxious for baptism, and the king wanted John to stay over Sunday and baptize. He could not do this, but promised to return in a fortnight, stay the Sunday, administer Holy Communion, and baptize those whom Mr. Lloyd should pronounce ready.

Chapter IX

AT WORK IN TORO

"Go ye and teach all nations, baptizing them in the name
of the Father, and of the Son, and of the Holy Ghost : . . -.
and, lo, I am with you alway, even unto the end of the
world."—*Matt.* xxviii. 19, 20.

A ND now the very last stage in the long
journey was reached. And this is John's
own account of his arrival at Kasagama's, which
took place on March 13th : " I was escorted by
three men sent by the king. About three hours
from Kasagama's I stopped for lunch in a beautiful
valley by a river, and, while here, several Baganda
teachers came running up from Kasagama's. We
hugged each other in true Baganda fashion. They
brought a note from Mr. Lloyd (the lay missionary
at Kasagama's), saying he would meet me later
(which he did, about a mile from the town).
My pen and note paper both fail to describe
my entry into Kasagama's. A lot of bright
hearty, strapping fellows met me at every corner.
They shouted and laughed. One saw I was

tired, and pushed me up the hill. The numbers increased every few minutes. The king, the Namasole (the king's mother), the ladies of the king's household (who wait on his wife and himself), all sent boy messengers to say 'Otyano.' These white-robed messengers with long sticks then rushed back to announce my arrival, and to say I greeted them. It was most embarrassing. The *coup de grace* was, however, when I met the ladies of the queen's household ! About a dozen of these buxom ladies rushed upon me, and, if Mr. Lloyd had not warned me, my hat, if not myself, would have been demolished. . . . There are wonderful signs of blessing, and many earnest Christians in these parts. All in front of us is the densest heathenism. No mission comes between us and the Congo (Baptist) Mission. At least one of the tribes within two days' march of us is cannibal. . . . We are in the very front of the fight, where I often longed to be. The Christians are warm, gentle souls, full of gratitude. Pray for them, and for me, that utterance may be given to preach the riches of Christ so as to be understood. I am VERY glad to be sent here. It is what I had often hoped for—to be placed where the Gospel has not been preached. The people are most warm-hearted. The king, Daudi (David), is a fine-looking man of twenty-one, but apparently much older. He is willing to build churches, preachers' houses, and do anything to help the work."

In his last letters to his mother John writes : " Just one line to say that I am really in Toro ! very safe and very sound, and very thankful. It is so jolly to feel a roof over my head again. Mr. Lloyd and I are living together. I like him already very much, and feel sure that we shall pull well together. We are right away from all other missionaries. An English official lives at a fort near with some Nubian troops, and there are, also, two French Roman Catholic priests in this capital of Kasagama's country. These are the only Europeans. Kasagama, the king, sent me a sheep on Saturday evening, as well as much matoke. It is a 'lady' sheep, so we are going to preserve her life in the hope that in due time she will present us with some lambs. Meat is sometimes scarce here, so it is well to have a flock, if possible. It is such a privilege to be out here, and I feel quite settled down. We have much fresh milk, butter, fowls, *English* potatoes, and some other English vegetables." And again : "It seems quite another

world to England. We have our kings and
chiefs, wars and tumults, peasantry, heathenism
and Christianity. The time passes very fast.
The mountains are glorious, and, now the rains
are beginning, the atmosphere is clearer. It
rains during this season one or two hours (or
more) each day and night. This morning, when
getting up at seven, it was very cold. The
people all get up much later than most Africans
because of the cold. . . . It is very wonderful to find so many round here who are just
waiting for the truth. I am sure that many
accounts of the missionary work have been much
exaggerated. It is, however, quite true that the
people everywhere seem to be 'waiting.' Most
nights we hear singing in houses close by, which
is done in honour of the heathen deity. I wrote
by last mail to Dr. Maxwell, asking him to print
some Toro Temperance Pledge Cards! The
people drink a very intoxicating liquor made
from banana juice fermented. . . . The climate here is really delightful, and I never remember feeling so fit in every way. It is, of
course, always warm during the day, but there
is always a breeze — sometimes quite bracing,
like sea air. The cool nights make it quite
possible to sleep, which it is very hard to do at

the coast and other parts of Africa. . . .
Long before this letter reaches you I hope to
be in the splendid mud-house which has been
built by Mr. Lloyd's directions and personal
work. It has three rooms. The thick thatch
roof is just finished, and a [number of Bunyoro
boys are covering the outside walls with some
white earth. It will look very much like a white
cottage in an English village."

On Sunday, March 21st, our dear young missionary celebrated the Holy Communion for the
first time in Luganda. Mr. Lloyd read the
prayers and preached. There were twenty communicants, including the king, his wife, and
his mother. The day before, at the weekly
Prayer Meeting, the king had prayed very simply
and earnestly for wisdom to guide his people.
His task was a very difficult one, as some of his
chiefs had been persuaded to become Roman
Catholics, and were in the habit of treating him
with but scant courtesy, at the instigation of their
religious advisers. When the king was baptized,
he took the Christian name of " David " in place
of his heathen name, " Kasagama." He wished
the name of his capital to be changed also, and
the hill on which his house stands is now called
Bethlehem—the City of David.

On Wednesday morning, March 24th, at 9.30, fourteen persons, including eight men, were baptized in the river. We cannot do better than give the description of this very striking episode in John's own words. He writes : "We had a most delightful service, and we felt it was a very real time of blessing. The king, his wife, his mother, and about 400 people, came to the river-side, and were seated on the high bank. We began with several hymns, and then, amid perfect silence, and a deep sense of the Divine Presence, I began to read the service. The candidates included several young chiefs, and some of the young girls of the Namasole's (king's mother's) household. They stood in front of the congregation, with their witnesses, to answer the questions, which they did most feelingly. While we sang a hymn, 'I am coming, Lord, coming now to Thee,' they walked round across a bridge a short distance to the opposite side of the river. I then baptized them, one by one, in mid-stream, and they passed to the congregation on the shore. It was a most intensely interesting service. Not only were the candidates themselves in real earnest, but *all* the congregation followed the service most devoutly. The glimpses of their faces from the river were wonderful. The Namasole embraced

the girls of her household in a most loving way—
greeting them afresh as true sisters in Christ. The
Namasole is a most sweet Christian soul, and her
influence is very great. The service ended with
the hymn, ' Oh happy day that fixed my choice,'
after which I gave the benediction, when the
big congregation went home with shouts—real
expressions of joy. I cannot express my thankfulness for this service—my first baptism in Africa!
The candidates mostly wore white clothes, and,
under the morning sun, we were soon all dry.
The place we chose for the baptism was close to
Captain Sitwell's fort, and he had most readily
given us permission to alter the banks a little.
The king had to call on him after the service, and,
to the inquiry whether he had had a good time
at the baptism, replied simply, ' Are not the
things of God all good ? ' "

On the afternoon of the same day, John started
with Mr. Lloyd for Mboga—a place five days'
march from the capital of Toro, on the borders of
Stanley's Great Forest—where there were ten converts reading for baptism. Two days after they
crossed the Semliki River in a long native " dug
out." This is a swift, deep river, about twenty-
five or thirty yards wide, infested by crocodiles
and hippopotami. At the different houses they

stayed they found charms and propitiatory offerings to the heathen deities. They made a halt
at the village of Buguma, on the west side of
the Ruwenzori range, as the chief had expressed
a desire to read " the Words of God." In his last
letter to his father, written at this place, John
says : "I used to think life out here would be
rather less full than at home, but the time seems
to pass even faster. We are always on the move,
and full of opportunities for work." He goes on
to speak of the difficulties raised by the Roman
Catholics in Toro. The senior priest had tried
to prejudice the king's mind against him by saying
that, unless the king left off reading with him, he
would perish eternally. Large gifts of cloth were
bestowed on chiefs and people to persuade them
to receive Baganda Roman Catholic teachers.
The priest had succeeded in turning out six
Protestant chiefs at Butiti, and the Protestant
king was in great distress at receiving an order
(inspired by him) from Captain Sitwell to re-
instate six Roman Catholic chiefs who had
voluntarily left him. " In spite of all these hin-
drances (John remarks), or is it because of them ?
the truth is rapidly spreading." An effort was
made to hold a service in Buguma, and the people
were invited to attend. But they all ran away.

HOUSE, TORO; THE RUWENZORI MOUNTAINS IN THE DISTANCE

They were afraid of the white men's "superstition." The next village reached belonged to the Baima tribe. This tribe is devoted to cow-keeping. Africans of other tribes do not understand cows, and will have nothing to do with them. Baima women of another tribe brought in food and water. They are poor degraded creatures, half-clad in skins. Their tribe is peculiar, as one that feeds on snakes. Many of these inhabit the native houses. Another tribe not far off is a cannibal tribe. These are the closing words of our dear brother's last circular letter : "The scenery this side of the Ruwenzori Mountains is most exquisite. I suppose very few Europeans have seen it. This morning we saw a great deal of snow on the highest peaks. We are in a plain lying between the Ruwenzori range and a lower range of hills on the west. We passed two worn-out volcanic craters on the road, and there are hot springs of boiling water at the foot of the Ruwenzori. The Roman Catholic Mission is a source of great trial to the work of Toro. Please pray for wisdom to know what to do."

Chapter X

" The sands of time are sinking,
The dawn of heaven breaks,
The summer morn I've sighed for,
The fair sweet morn awakes.
Dark, dark hath been the midnight,
But day-spring is at hand,
And glory, glory dwelleth
In Emmanuel's land."
                                        —*Cousins.*

" Except a corn of wheat fall into the ground and die, it abideth alone ; but if it die, it bringeth forth much fruit."—*St. John* xii. 24.

THE end of a devoted life was now drawing near. The keynote of that life is struck by those beautiful words found upon the flyleaf of Eustace Maxwell's Bible in the wreck of the train which called him to his early crown,—

"Just as I am—young, strong, and free,
To be the best that I can be
For Truth and Righteousness and Thee,
Lord of my life, I come."

If there was one thing that shone out more than

another in our dear brother's character, it was
the humble, trustful, happy spirit in which he
met all that befell him.   He is always writing of
thankfulness, joy, privilege.   His work, however
arduous, was his constant refreshment and delight.
When appointed to Toro, his first impulse seems
rather to have been a feeling of a little diffident
surprise that one so young and inexperienced as
he was should be sent to so remote and difficult
a post.   But he took it directly as God's will
and the answer to prayer, and cheerfully began
at once all needful preparation.   Looking at his
story from a mere human point of view, it would
seem sad and mysterious that there should have
been that long journey, during all those weary
months, with all that effort to learn the language,
and then only a very few short weeks of actual
labour.   It is, indeed, a very touching thing
when God thus accepts, otherwise than in the
manner of its offering, the sacrifice of a young
and devoted life !   Faith assures us that all was
just as it should be.   The self-sacrifice and self-
denial (which must have been great, although we
do not read much of it in his letters) was all
swallowed up in the gladness of God's felt Presence,
and of the tokens of favour and success which He
now and again graciously vouchsafed to him.

His short spell of missionary work made the happiest part of his life. God gave him a sweet taste of the work he had so longed for, and then called his loving spirit home to an eternal rest. We can say of him in those striking words of the Book of Wisdom (iv. 13, 14) : " He being made perfect in a short time, fulfilled a long time —for his soul pleased the Lord ; therefore hasted He to take him away." And this was the way in which the Home Call came to him. We quote the graphic letter of Mr. Lloyd to his father. Mr. Lloyd had been to him a most faithful, useful, and loving helper, and ministered to him most devotedly (as will be seen) in his last moments. The letter is dated April 26th, from Bamutenda, Toro. " The saddest of all tasks has now fallen to my lot. It is to give you a detailed account of the last few days of your devoted son ; and I pray that, as you read of the last few moments of the life of one so dear to you, God may give you His most loving sympathy, and that the healing oil of His love may be applied. Surely there is nothing that should so fill us with holy hopefulness as the triumphant death of a saint of God. My beloved brother reached this place in the middle of the month of March, and my joy at welcoming such a companion as my fellow-

worker could hardly be exaggerated. Since I got
to this place, a year ago, I have been very much
alone, and have often longed for a fellow-worker,
who would be really a help to me, and with whom
I could commune in spirit ; and all this I found
in my dear brother, your son. Soon after he
arrived here, we were called to go to our furthest
outpost, Mboga, as there were there thirteen
candidates awaiting baptism. I went part of the
way with him, but had to return, as the work at
Toro (the capital) could not be left. After a fortnight's visit, Callis returned, and seemed in good
spirits and very well. He rested two days, holding Baptism Services here, and then went off to
Mwenge, a place about twenty-five miles away,
where we have a house, church, and a large, en-
couraging work going on. He arrived in rather
a tired condition, having sent for some of the
natives to help him in, which they did, bringing
a hammock and carrying him. The following day
the chief of the place wrote to me, asking me for
medicine for Callis, who was ill. Instead of
sending medicine, I at once (although it was three
o'clock in the afternoon, and twenty-five miles
lay between us) set out on my bicycle ' Speed
away,' and did the twenty-five miles in three hours.
I found my dear brother in a sad way, his

temperature at 108°. He was also very sick, and, what surprised me most, he was out of bed. Poor dear fellow, he little knew the power of fever, as we get it out here. He said, 'Oh, Lloyda (this is what he always called me), 'why have you come all this way? I am not really ill, only a little tired!' I got him at once to bed, but he begged me not to trouble myself on his behalf, but to get food and go to bed after my long ride. I told him I had come to nurse him, and he must do what I told him, and a tear sparkled in his eye as he said, 'I shall soon be all right.' (Yes! dear brother, soon all right in Jesus' bosom!) That night the dear fellow suffered very much, but, through it all, was most patient, and his constant remark was: 'Don't trouble, dear Lloyda.' On Saturday he seemed much better and wanted to get up; but I urged him to keep quiet, and I sat and read a few chapters to him, and we also sang together a few hymns, and then he slept until Sunday morning. I was by his bedside when he awoke, and could not but praise God to see my beloved companion so much better. I begged him to keep his bed, and I sat with him during the day. It was Easter Sunday, of all days in the year the most glorious. He asked me to sing to him :—

'On the Resurrection morning
Soul and body meet again ;
No more sorrow, no more weeping,
No more pain.'

"He lay quite quiet until I reached the last line
of the last verse, and then, with all his strength,
he joined me in that one line : 'Waking up in
Christ's own likeness, *satisfied*.' After that hymn
he lay quite still, and seemed asleep, so I left
him a few moments, and went into the next room,
and I heard him when I had gone just pouring out
his whole soul to God in such prayer as we seldom
hear. It was only meant for his dear Saviour's
ears ; but I could not help listening ; it seemed to
bring God so near. Towards evening, fever came on
and reached a very high temperature, and on that
day I sat by him bathing his fevered brow and
putting cold water to his parched lips. Once he
almost shouted, 'O my God, I can't bear it.' I
leant over him and said, 'Jesus can help you
to bear it.' It was a magic word to him, for he
started, and then a smile came over his face, and
he closed his eyes and was quite still. In the
morning the fever abated again, and he took
a little nourishment. Monday, Tuesday, and
Wednesday he was quieter, and seemed to be
getting on well, and very little fever showed itself. Wednesday morning he was particularly

11

bright, and we sat and talked together. First I
read to him John v., and he said a few words
upon verses 25, 28, 29, mentioning the reference
to the two Resurrections—that which now is, and
that which is to come. Then he asked me to
sing to him again, and I did so, he himself
choosing the hymns. His choice was curious.
'Days and moments quickly flying' was one of
the first; 'We shall sleep, but not for ever,' and
then 'Abide with me, fast falls the eventide.'
He really seemed much better, and his temperature was low. Alas! it was the calm before the
storm. I left him a moment to get some food
in the next room, and he continued singing; first
he sang,—

> 'The sands of time are sinking,
> The dawn of Heaven breaks.
> The summer morn I've sighed for,
> The fair sweet morn awakes.'

" I was much struck with the *power* he put into
it. For a few moments he was quiet, and then he
sang, 'Peace, perfect peace,' and at the fifth verse
he stopped. You remember the words :—

> 'Peace, perfect peace, our future all unknown ;
> Jesus we know, and He is on the throne.'

" I thought he had fallen asleep, and in a few
moments I walked to his bedside, and was

amazed to see him with his eyes wide open, lying
on his side. I spoke to him, but he neither
moved nor spoke, and I knew he was quite un-
conscious. I took his temperature, and found it
very high indeed. I covered him up with blankets,
having previously given him medicine, and then
waited, hoping soon to see him revive. All night
I sat with him, with a little boy with me. Oh,
what could I do! I was so helpless, and yet
my heart was breaking. No return of consciousness came. As soon as it was light I sent for
help, and two or three Baganda came to help
me. Our first thing was to bathe him in cool
water, then we sat still and waited, just moving
him from side to side, and applying cold water
to his head and neck ; but all in vain. All that
day, Thursday, there was absolutely no change,
as far as man could see ; but I somehow felt that
I was at the bedside of a dying man. Oh, what
hours of agony those were! I could not leave
his side (for 106 hours I never left him, not even
for sleep). On Friday a change came, a much
higher temperature, and not for one moment did
his eyes close for sleep,—just that terrible, vacant
stare. Once he fixed his eyes on me, and it
seemed as though he recognised me. I bent
over him and just called him by name, and for

a moment there was the slightest sign of returning consciousness; but it was gone instantly,
nor did it return.

"We did all in our power to bring him round;
but we were helpless: the call had come. Friday
night I shall never forget. The chief and many
natives had gathered together in the house, knowing the end was near. The chief's sister, who
had seemed devoted to him in life, sat at the
head of the bed, bathing him with cold water
and wiping the death dew from his brow. One
woman's tender care and loving attention he had
right to the end. Towards morning, about five
o'clock, we all saw death was very near. I
called the people in, and we prayed together, so
far as sobs would let us, and then his heavy
breathing was the only sound heard. All waited
in breathless silence for the end. At last it came.
My candle, which was by his bedside, flickered,
and then went out, and almost at the same
moment my beloved brother fell asleep, and the
first rays of the morning sun flashed into the
room, and the birds then burst forth into song,
as the victor passed into the courts of the King,
into endless day, to be for ever with the Lord.
Instinctively we all fell upon our knees, and we
had five minutes' silent prayer, broken only by

the stifled sobs of all present. I then, with the help of the Muganda teacher, performed the last service to the tired body. The chief sent down twelve yards of fine white linen, and in this we wrapped him, and, on the outside, one of my blankets on which he breathed his last. It was when this was done that I shed the first tears of my manhood, and I wept like a little child, not for the one who had gone, but for the awful feeling of loneliness which seemed to overwhelm me. But Jesus poured in the healing balm, and I was able to look up into the face of my never-failing Friend and say, ' Thy will be done.' We chose a nice little spot for his grave close by the church, and here I buried him. And as I read, before a vast crowd of heathen and Christians combined, the glorious Burial Service, hope seemed to spring up within my heart, and I left the graveside feeling stronger. And so we laid him to rest with the blessed hope of a glorious resurrection. I cannot add more, but will write again when I send to you the few little things he has left behind that I feel sure you will like to have. May God, our dear Father of all com-fort, comfort you, and make you entirely sub-missive to His dear will. With kindest Christian love and sympathy."

Mr. and Mrs. Callis were spending their holiday at Felixstowe, when the sad news of their sudden and unexpected loss was conveyed to them in a letter, full of deep sympathy (dated August 5th), from Mr. Marshall Lang, Lay Secretary of the C.M.S., in the absence of his clerical colleague—a cablegram having reached the Society from Zanzibar: " Callis asleep. Toro. May." He writes : " We mourn the early removal of one to whom we looked as a leader in the work in Uganda, and whose offer of service was so lately accepted with much satisfaction. We can only unite with you in praying that this unexpected blow may, in God's inscrutable Providence, be rather for the furtherance of the cause, in leading others to fill the gap caused by your son's early call to his reward. I am aware that your son was engaged ; please communicate the tidings to the lady, with whose grief we truly sympathize."

The Rev. H. E. Fox, Secretary of the Society writes :—

" BUNCRANA, LONDONDERRY,
                    " *August* 20*th*, 1897.
"DEAR MR. CALLIS,—
    " I have been away from papers and letters, and have but lately heard of the sore loss which has fallen chiefly on you, and next on us and the Church of Christ. Yet where could a soldier of the Cross choose a better place to

be found when his Master calls him than in the very fore-
front of the battle ?   To us it seems strange that one just
beginning to give proof of his powers as a missionary,
and already making the influence of his holy life felt,
should be summoned away from the work where he seemed
to be so much needed ; but the Master knew best, and
your dear son has entered into the joy of his Lord, to hear
the ' Well done, good and faithful servant,' as surely as to
the oldest veteran.

"You may be sure that many are remembering you and
yours in this bereavement with deep sympathy and constant prayer, and among them not least,

"Yours most sincerely,

"H. E. Fox, *Hon. Sec.*

"REV. J. CALLIS."

At a Committee Meeting of the C.M.S., which
met shortly afterwards, the following Resolution
was ordered to be entered on the Minutes :—

"That the Committee have heard, with sincere
regret, that the Society has lost a young Missionary, whose work gave promise of much future
usefulness, in the removal by death of the Rev.
John Samuel Callis, on the very threshold of his
work in Uganda, and only three months after
his arrival in that country. Your Committee
note the fact that, with the exception of the
death of Bishop Hannington by violence, this is
the first death of one of the Society's missionaries which has occurred north of the Victoria
Nyanza.   After graduating at Cambridge, and

receiving further theological training at Wycliffe Hall, Oxford, Mr. Callis, while Curate of All Saints', Woolwich, offered to the Society in June, 1896, for work in Uganda. He reached that country in the February of the present year, and was located in Toro. The Committee desire that an expression of their sympathy in the heavy bereavement which the family and friends of Mr. Callis are thus called upon to bear, in the Providence of God, should be conveyed to his father, the Rev. J. Callis, and to his *fiancée*, Miss Baker."

A very large number of letters of condolence, expressive of the highest appreciation of the dear departed, poured in upon the bereaved parents, and helped them greatly to bear up under the heavy blow.

Bishop Tucker writes, under date of August 9th: "Your letter of a week or two ago told of cheerful brightness and lively hopes, and now all is changed, and the first of all our missionary band to be laid to rest in the country won for our Lord north of the Lake is your dear son. One can only say, 'The Lord's will be done,' and pray earnestly that it may be given to you, and all near and dear to him who is gone, to know in your heart that 'He is doing all

things well,' and that He is saying to you in
this hour of your sorrow, 'What I do thou
knowest not now, but thou shalt know here-
after.' I pray, indeed, that much of the realized
Presence of our Lord may be yours, and that
He who is the God of all comfort and the very
Consolation of Israel may pour into your hearts
that peace and comfort which He alone can
impart. Pray accept the expression of my
deepest, truest sympathy, and believe that much
prayer will be offered up for you by those who
know what it is to suffer on this behalf."

Archdeacon Walker (of Uganda) writes how
much all out there valued him, and how well they
got to know him in the short time he was with
them. He adds : " It was a great comfort to feel
that we had such a man in Toro, for Toro is a
difficult place to work in. Many difficulties are
sure to arise, and, as Toro is eight or ten days'
from Mengo, often the brethren have to act on
their own judgment, without referring the matter
to Mengo. With Callis there, we all had such
confidence that the best would always be done
under the circumstances, whatever they might be.
Lloyd, too, wrote thanking us for sending such a
good man to work with him. . . . It has
pleased God to take Callis after a very short

term of service here ; one can only feel of such
a man, 'May my last end be like his!' It
seems a long way to have walked all out here,
and then to lie down and die after some two
months in the country. It is difficult to understand why such a useful man in every way
should be taken."

Mr. Baskerville, who travelled most of the way
with him, and who, as will be remembered, is
frequently mentioned by dear John in his letters,
writes of him : " He was a man who lived very
near to Christ, and *the* best, I think, of this
year's party." " There is one very heavy piece
of news to tell, and that is the death of Callis
in Toro. He was of the cream of this last party,
and now has gone. One can hardly write of
other things alongside of this."

Dr. A. R. Cook, whose name also frequently
occurs in this memoir, writes : " He endeared
himself greatly to us. His steadfastness of purpose, highness of resolve, and whole-hearted missionary consecration, was only equalled by the
transparent character of his life. I shall feel grateful to the end of my life for having known him.
His sermon at Nandi on 'The Living Christ'
was an inspiration to us, and will live long in
our memories. Your son was eminently one who

'. . . never turned his back, but marched breast for-
    ward,
  Never doubted clouds would break,
  Never dreamed, though right were worsted, wrong would
    triumph,
  Held—we fall to rise, are baffled to fight better, sleep
    to wake.

'No—at noontide in the bustle of men's work time
  Greet the unseen with a cheer !
  Bid him forward, breast or back, as either should be,
  "Strive and thrive" cry "Speed—fight on—fare ever
    There as here."'

I want to let you know that, though I was
not privileged to attend your son in his last
illness, Mr. Lloyd treated him with much skill,
and I don't suppose the result would have been
very different if I had been there. His home-
call evidently came from the Master, and 'when
he heard that, he arose quickly and went unto
Him.'"

Mr. Clayton, who was one of the missionary
party and the most intimate with him, refers in
his letter to the above-mentioned striking sermon.
He particularly notes also the infinite pains he
took with the one Christian Muganda amongst
the porters—having him in his tent every afternoon, and reading and explaining the Bible to
him. He writes: "We all felt that he lived
nearer to God, perhaps, than any of us, and was

the most ready to go home. He used to say, on his voyage out, that the one thing he wanted was to '*know God*.' He has now got his wish, and gone in to see the King in His beauty."

Miss Taylor, another of the party, whose name frequently appears in John's letters, writes to his father thus : " We who travelled up here with Mr. Callis know a little of what he was—a man who truly lived in the Presence of God. We always, felt it a privilege and source of strength to have a little talk with him, and we thank God for letting us know him amidst the strange circumstances of Safari life."

Mr. Lloyd, senr., writes : " Your beloved son seemed almost to belong to us, for our dear Albert had written of him in such affectionate terms, and the knowledge that they were united in the great work to which God had called them, made us feel a very special regard for him, although we had never seen him."

Canon Garratt gives a few interesting reminiscences of the time immediately preceding his missionary life. He says that he was evidently taking a very deep interest in the subject of our Lord's Second Coming ; that, as his mind had been passing through a good deal of conflict as to the foundations of the faith, his interest in a subject

so objective in its nature was a proof how complete had been the victory. John thus refers to a
visit made by Canon Garratt to Woolwich in one
of his letters in which this subject was handled:
" Every one enjoyed his time here. He most
kindly came to my rooms and gave a lecture
on the historical and futurist views of prophecy.
About twelve men formed the congregation, and
we had a delightful time." Canon Garratt felt
that he was going out to the mission field under
no illusion, but in a Scriptural spirit, to do the
Master's work until He should come Himself to
complete it. He adds: " His general bearing, his
thoughtful energy, his firm and quiet tones,
struck me much. I thought he had a great
work before him—and so, indeed, he had, though
not exactly as I anticipated. But it cannot be
doubted that, in increasing missionary interest at
home, and laying the foundation of the Church
in Toro, he did more by his death than most
men do by their lives."

The Bishop of Southwark, writing to his father,
recalls the fact that it was at his house that John
spent the Ember days before his ordination. He
formed a very warm admiration for him. He believed that he would be very valuable in English
work, and more than once spoke to him of it,

pleading that there was a great mission field of
exceptional difficulty amongst the lapsed of South
London ; but his heart was fixed. The Bishop
adds : " He has won his mission crown, while we
still remain, not yet sufficiently proved. . . . I
do trust that these few words from one who was
much concerned with the great epoch of his life
may do something, by the mercy of God, to
lead you to the greatest comfort of all—I mean
the strong belief that he offered himself to our
blessed Lord, and that that offer has been accepted to the fullest extent."

From his distant holiday resort at the Riffel
Alp, the Dean of Norwich sends this touching
message : " My heart is sore for you and dear
Mrs. Callis. God the Holy Ghost be very near
to you in all His tenderness and in gentlest
power. Life is measured, not by years, but by
love ; in this your dear son was old, and old before
his time. Yet I do grieve for you."

From Scotland Archdeacon Perowne writes :—

" It is indeed mysterious that a life so full of promise,
and a work bidding so fair to unfold on earth, should be
brought, as it seems to us, to so untimely a close. And
yet we are sure (God give us faith to hold it fast !) that
life and work have reached alike their highest goal and
their noblest development. You gave him to the Lord
when first He gave him to you, and now He, the Great

Prophet, has said to you yet again, 'Give me thy son, and has borne him away for a little while into His secret chamber, only that He may bring him forth to you again for ever, and say, 'See, thy son liveth !

"He has joined the noble army of martyrs, who, in Uganda and throughout the great Mission field, have loved not their lives unto the death for His Name's sake.

"God bless and comfort and support you and yours, and her who more than shares with you the desolation of this great loss.

" In all kindest sympathy,

"I am, yours very sincerely,

"T. T. PEROWNE."

Miss Brophy, writing from Salisbury Square, says : " In a letter received from Uganda yesterday, from Miss Timpson, one of the ladies who went to Uganda in the same party, she writes : 'I did rejoice when it was settled that Mr. Callis should go to Toro, and we all expected great things from him. To know him was to know more of God, and one felt how he lived continually in the Presence of Jesus. His life was a true testimony, and one thanks God for it. All felt what a loss it was to the Mission, and yet we know " It is well." ' " Miss Brophy continues : " I feel sure that this *unofficial*, earnest testimony to your son's life and influence will be precious to you all. One does see how God's richest blessing seems to come down on the fields in which the early labourers are sleeping, and it may be that God has great purposes of blessing for Toro from the death there of one who had hoped to *live* for the people."

His first vicar, Mr. Talbot Rice, writes, after expressing his own and his wife's deep sympathy with the bereaved parents: "I was very fond of him during the little while we were together, and was very sorry to have to leave him. His energy, zeal, and devotion to the Master and to the working people was delightful and contagious. A great many owe much to him. He was so thoroughly anxious to do anything new which might awaken some. I loved him, and I am sure the people did. Dear Mr. Jukes was particularly fond of him, and several times spoke to me of his devotion to the work."

This is the veteran Mr. Jukes' own testimony: " The whole parish is mourning. For your beloved son, in a very special and unusual degree, endeared himself to the congregation here as very few curates do, while his life was a sermon to us all. I feel as if for a while I had lost a son. Ever since he left us he has been constantly on my heart. Now he is gone before us, and, while we cannot but grieve to have lost him, we cannot but rejoice also for his sake ; for he is not really lost to us, but will be surely serving us yet in

the unity of the Body of Christ. Christ in spirit
is not far from us, but yet serves us. Why should
not His members do the same, though in the
flesh we do not see them ? Not a day passes
that I do not think of your dear John. Why
should he not think of us ? I wonder whether
you are doing anything to have a stone put up
to mark the place where his mortal remains are
lying. Such memorials of the Gospel pioneers
who have taken the Gospel to Africa will, in a
few years, be really valuable, and a voice to the
natives, telling them at what cost the blessed
Gospel was brought to them. Dear John has
given his life for Christ, and I feel sure that his
death, even as his life, will be a blessing to many.
He left marks here which can never be effaced.
I cannot add more, I am suffering so much from
rheumatism that it is very difficult for me to write
a line ; but I cannot hear of the departure of
your dear son without trying to express my truest
and deepest sympathy with you and his mother."

Mr. Morris, who, it will be remembered, succeeded Mr. Talbot Rice as vicar of All Saints',
Plumstead, writes : " Since Saturday night one has
been in a kind of dream. I find it so hard to realize
and to understand—my dear colleague—my first—
and your dear son gone ! Yesterday was a day to

12

be remembered in All Saints'. All in church were moved when I read your letter at the beginning of the service. In the morning we sung 'My God, my Father', and 'Who are these like stars appearing?' and in the evening, 'What are these in bright array?' 'Why should I fear?' and 'Peace, perfect peace,' which fitted in with my text, 'The peace of God which passeth all understanding shall keep your hearts and minds.' His life was a short one, his ministry quite brief, but they told for good. His example of self-sacrifice at the time of the typhoid epidemic will never be forgotten here. He helped working men in a quite singular degree. Oh, how little the plans and projects we make seem when face to face with a sorrow like this, and yet how real does the spirit world become! Dear Mr. Jukes, of whom he who has gone before was so fond, feels the blow greatly. All that sympathy and prayer can give we do indeed give. Some day I hope we shall see you. Always will you be welcomed here for your own sake, and above all for the sake of him who helped to make many of us more Christlike, less selfish."

Mrs. Morris writes to his mother: "I wept that we should see your dear son's face no more. I always pictured him returning to tell us of his work, and we receiving him so proudly as our own peculiar missionary. We had sad services yesterday,—though the note of triumph was also there ; but many tears were shed, for he has many true and loving friends at All Saints', who remember gratefully his good work here. You and he are much in our thoughts and prayers that the God of all comfort may be with you. It ·must be a great comfort to you even now, in the midst of all your grief, to think of his noble, self-sacrificing life, and how he has now laid it down for the sake of his Master."

The Rev. F. J. Chavasse writes : " The news from Central Africa has almost stunned me, and my heart, since I heard it, has been constantly going out towards and up for you and Mrs. Callis. We cannot understand, we can only rest in the character of God, and wait. He is too wise to make any mistake. He loves too much to hurt needlessly. Some day He will make all plain, and we shall praise Him for what seems at present an insoluble mystery. God can feel specially with you. He gave His Son to die for men : you have given your son to lay down his life for Africa. You have offered him your best, and He cannot fail to comfort and bless you. It is one of the great laws of His kingdom that we gain by losing, and your dear boy's home call may bring untold blessings on you, your family, God's people, the Church, and Africa. To-day he holds Toro for Christ, and his zeal will provoke many. Be sure that the Lord, Whom sorrow attracts, will be near to comfort you and yours. He is leading you along the path He has trodden with His own feet. He Himself went not up to joy, but first He suffered pain. He entered not into His glory before He was crucified."

The Rev. E. Millar writes : " I was one of the two last people, now in England, to see Callis in Uganda. I was much struck by his calmness and peacefulness. He seemed to be one of those who take things quietly, knowing that God will bring all things out as He sees best, and being content to wait for it. I had hoped that the infant Church in Toro would be much helped by his advice and guiding ; now, perhaps, it will be helped by his glorifying God by his death. He seemed to us to be just the man for that most difficult post— one who would not act rashly, but would well weigh his words and actions. The work which he had to do in Toro, in the face of much opposition from the Romanists, from the Government officials, and from the heathen, was by no means an easy one; whilst the king Kasagama, although anxious to serve God, seems in some points to have been a little ill-advised in his actions. We hoped that your son would prove a tower of strength to him."

Mr. Fisher writes: "I do not remember ever hearing anything which gave me a greater shock than the sad telegram announcing the death of your dear son, and our dear comrade and fellow-worker. We all said at Mengo that he was the man for Toro, strongest—spiritually, mentally and physically—for that most important post. I saw a letter from my old comrade Lloyd, written since the arrival of your son in Toro, and it was full of praise to God that such a man had been sent him. Poor fellow! he will feel the blow, and the dear natives also."

The Editor of the C.M. *Gleaner* sends this message : " I need not tell you how we all mourned the loss of one so promising and so early removed. He was a ' sower ' indeed ; but he had at least the privilege of beginning to sow in real earnest. To have been able to minister to the people in their own tongue, and to have taken part in some of the in-gathering—these are privileges which we may be thankful were accorded to him, before he was called to the higher ministry above."

The Rev. J. W. Marshall, the father of one of the Ku Cheng martyrs, writes :—

" HÔTEL BRISTOL,
" AIX-LES-BAINS,
"*August* 19*th*, 1897.

" MY DEAR MR. CALLIS,—

" I have been feeling very much with you the last few days, and should like to write and tell you so. We gave our children to Christ for His work, as He saw fit to use them. He has accepted our gift, and seen fit to call them to rest after a very short period of work in the fields to which they had dedicated their lives. We know that He has done well, wisely, and lovingly for them, for us, and for the work ; but still this knowledge does not stay or mitigate our grief. The only mitigation I find—and it is a very real one—is in the contemplation of the place of rest, and the state of rest in which they are who are ' *with Him.*' Then I, for one, would not have her back. I doubt not, dear friend, that you and your wife will find the same alleviation in your sorrow.

" I feel most intensely for Miss Baker, and have tried to write a few words of sympathy to her.

" Believe me,
" Your sincere friend,
" J. W. MARSHALL."

Canon Robinson, of Norwich, Master of St. Catharine's College, writes : " I have heard with the deepest regret of the death of your dear son, which was mentioned in the Cathedral both by Canon Collett and myself. It is a pathetic end to a very promising life, just as the day of great usefulness was dawning upon him, and as he was looking forward to a happy future in union with one in sympathy with him and his work. All this is very mysterious. You and your dear wife will feel that the natural order of life is reversed as you—and not he—are left to mourn. But it may be that the sorrow felt all around for him, and the high opinion held of him and of the work he was expected to do, may be some help to you both in your trouble. God has laid His hand heavily upon you in the past years, and He must have some still greater work for which He is preparing you. He has enabled you to bear your great sorrows with faith and patience, and I am convinced He will give you the strength required for a trial which, at first, must seem to you both to blot out all the sunshine from your life. . . . I feel that he is one of our members who has done us honour in the best sense, and whom the College will be thankful to have had once on a time enrolled amongst them."

The Rev. Canon Ripley writes: "Your news is quite overwhelming to us both. Mrs. Ripley prayed for him every day. The danger to life seemed, too, so little in Uganda compared with other Missionary spheres. But while nature will mourn, what a blessed thought that he has already finished his course with joy—so bright an example! The first white man's grave in Toro, taking possession (as old Mr. Krapf said about his wife) for Christ!" Mrs. Ripley adds: "Dear, dear Friends, I can only weep; it is too, too touchingly affecting—to us disappointing."

The late venerable Rev. F. Fitch, of Cromer, writes: "We have the unspeakable consolation that our dear children, who so willingly gave themselves to the Master's service on earth, are now called to higher service; and we a little longer wait (it was but a very little longer with the dear writer)[1] to join them in that blessed home where God will wipe all tears from our eyes."

Miss M. Fitch mentions that Bishop Oluwole made the most touching allusion in Cromer Parish Church to dear John before a crowded congregation, and, appealing for helpers, quoted from that beautifully compiled card which his father had sent with the son's last words, speaking also so feelingly of those who had gone from Norfolk.

The Rev. A. E. Barnes Lawrence sent the accompanying sympathizing and appreciative words: "My wife and I have been greatly dis-

---

[1] Mr. Fitch died September 7th, within a month of writing the above, after fifty-three years' faithful ministry.

tressed to-day to learn that your dear son has laid down his life in Uganda. I had a real regard for him, coupled with a very high opinion of his spiritual life and whole-hearted surrender to Christ. His offer of service was not surprising, for it was of a piece with his life. Dear fellow! he would not have had it otherwise, except for the sake of those he loved. It marks the beginning of an endless service, on which he has entered sooner than we could have anticipated. His life, short as it was, was by no means in vain. He was influential for Christ among many (including ourselves). He never thought he helped, and it is good to think of his reward. For yourself, you have given the Lord your best ; there is nothing too precious for *Him*."

Canon Girdlestone writes : " The calamity is great for the Mission body, and for those amongst whom your dear boy was beginning to work ; but, after all, it is greatest for the parents. Whenever I read of John the Baptist's end, at the age of about thirty-one or thirty-two, I feel that it is in line with what has now happened. So, in the case of Stephen, and, perhaps, of James, the brother of John. The enemy seems to prevail against the chosen of God. One thinks that God could have intervened on behalf of James, as He did in the case of Peter. God could certainly have refused permission to Satan to touch your boy's life, as He did in the case of Job. We are on the edge of a great mystery here, which I think Scripture does not solve. But there is another side to it. The migration from this world to the spirit-world no more removes your boy from the arms of Christ than did his migration from England to Toro. 'Lord both of the dead and of the living. All live unto Him!' It is this which one clings to with regard to the present, and there is a glorious hope in the future."

The Rev. F. Storer Clark, Vicar of St. Peter's, Greenwich, writes : "'The Lord gave; blessed be the name of the Lord.' It was indeed a gracious boon to have had such a son and brother ; yea, still to have him, for 'he being dead, yet speaketh.' His life lives on in the hearts and lives, not merely of fond relatives and attached friends, but also at Plumstead, Uganda, and elsewhere. Thankfulness for the past is a help for the rent soul so keenly feeling the gap to add, 'The Lord hath taken away; blessed be the name of the Lord.' . . . There are and will be happy reunions, as well as grievous partings."

Mr. H. W. Young, of Blackheath, under whose roof John stayed at the time of his Ordination to the priesthood, writes : "From what we then saw of him, I feel sure that it is as he would wish—to close his life in active service—and he has been early taken to his reward."

The Rev. E. Symonds, John's brother-in-law, whose happy intercourse with him at Keswick has already been recorded, sends these words of cheer to the bereaved mother : "The contents of Mr. Lloyd's letter give us a grand triumph of faith, and, with that thought uppermost, the sadness cannot find place. It is the victor's end, yea the beginning of life. 'When the fruit is *ripe, immediately,*' etc. Oh ! that we were *ripe*, and lived, as he did, more as citizens of heaven, and less as those of earth. Mr. Head (then Vicar of Christ Church, Hampstead) has brought us a circular letter from Dr. Cook, in which he says : ' He was eminently a choice spirit, and we all got much attached to him on the march up country. Will you send some one from Christ Church to fill up the gap ?' They have got a new hospital at Mengo ; Dr. Cook appeals for those who will support a bed. Two of the twelve have been taken—£4 a year. Could we not take up one in memory of one so dear ? I will, with many, gladly find help."

This admirable suggestion was thankfully taken

up at once. In a letter dated September 15th,
Dr. A. H. Cook—brother of Dr. Cook at Mengo
—writes to John's father : " Permit me to thank
you and Mrs. Callis most warmly, on my brother's
behalf, for your kind offer to endow a Bed in
my brother's hospital in Mengo in memory of
your son. Will you also convey my thanks to the
Rev. E. Symonds and his wife for their kind
thought? I will write by the next mail to in-
form my brother of your generous gift, and of
your wish that the Bed should be named in
memory of your son, and I am sure his wishes
will be identical with ours in this matter. Personally I do not think any one could choose a
more fitting memorial of your son's noble missionary efforts than in endowing a Bed in his
name."

We add a few words taken from a letter of
Elizabeth Farrow, Parish Nurse of All Saints':
" I know there will be much sorrow in the parish
at these sad tidings. I trust it may awaken
some to remember the faithful warning words
he spoke to them, and to them may his voice
still speak ! I think of him in his love for
prayer, and the longing, yearning pleading for
more holiness of life. I believe there will be
much consolation to you and all his loved ones

to know God appointed that he should have a loving Christian helper by him all through his illness, one of whom the Master will say, ' I was sick and ye visited ME,' and who will 'in no wise lose his reward.' I do thank God Mr. Lloyd was with him. May many be found who will respond to the appeal which comes from the outstretched hands of the hungering and thirsting people in Toro, and go over and take up the work of him who has had the call, ' Come up higher.' . . . No wonder he left the earth *singing*—for he loved singing."

From a Missionary in Manitoba, who knew dear John at Cambridge and worked in Mission work with him, there came a little card with these words: "Let this card bear to you the assurance of true sympathy from one who commends you in your sorrow to the care of the Infinite Father, Who fain would be your strength and comfort now, and at the last wipe away all tears!"

In concluding this Memoir there seem to be no words more appropriate than those brief but pregnant ones of the Apostle St. Paul in I Cor. xv. 10 : "Not I, but the grace of God which was with me." It is most deeply interesting to mark the operation of that Divine grace in the thoughts, and the life-work of our dear departed brother.

We see how it transformed a naturally retiring, somewhat reserved character into one aglow with love and zeal, full of holy resolution, power, and intense earnestness. We see it appointing and over-ruling inward struggles and conflicts and doubts to the making of a seasoned soldier of the Cross. We see how it wrought in him that profound humility which scarcely ever permits him in his letters to speak of *himself.* We see how it made him a man of one aim—to preach and live and glorify Christ. This Memoir is not written for the sake of exalting the man or his work, but of exalting the Holy Spirit of Christ, Who dwelt and worked in him. It is hardly possible for an earnest-minded reader to avoid asking himself the question: "Might *I* not, through the same grace, live a more devoted, consecrated, useful, Christ-like life? Might I not realize more of the joy of fellowship and service?" Nay, more, perhaps a further question: "May *I* not fill his place in the Mission field? 'Lord, here am I; send me!'"

WANTED!

A sower has fallen in the field,
Where his work had but just begun;
It seemed to us but the sunrise to him,
When we heard that his work was done.
But who will take up the sowing now,

To scatter the good living seed,
And carefully tend through its growing time,
And root up the noxious weed?
A reaper has laid his sickle down,
The Master has called him away;
We thought he had many hours to toil,
Night came to him, whilst it was day!
And who will take up the sickle now
And reap in that white harvest field,
And gather the golden grain for Him,
Whose is the abundant yield?
A voice is stilled, so lately heard
Proclaiming the Gospel's call,
Telling so joyfully Heaven's good news,
Of a Saviour who died for all!
Who will take up the herald's note
And preach God's goodwill towards men,
And thus will help to prepare the way
For that Saviour's coming again?
"'Tis true," said the worker lately gone,
That "Dark Africa waiteth still."
Many hands are there stretched out to God.
Who will go for the Lord? Who will?

FELIXSTOWE,   J. C.
August, 1897.

Mr. Morris says in the All Saints' Magazine:
"What more glorious end can there be to a Christian's earthly life than the laying it down for the
Master's sake in the Master's cause? Will not the
thought of our dear friend—his life—his death—
help to prevent us giving way to self, or indolence,
or spiritual apathy? Very striking now, in the
light of what has happened, is it to read the

words of his farewell text (St. John xii. 24). God
grant that his death may not deter others from
going to the Mission-field, and from facing danger,
but rather be to them a more direct call than
they have had before. The soldier of the Queen
does not fear danger because a comrade falls in
battle. Shall the soldier of the Cross be less
loyal or less true?"

Mr. A. B. Fisher, in a powerful address at the
All Saints' Gleaners' Union, mentioned that at his
meeting with his dear departed brother at Mengo,
he gave him this charge: "Go to the people at
Plumstead and tell them all that has been done
for Toro." Mr. Fisher did so in these words.

"Two years ago the King of Toro wondered
what had come to Uganda people, saying at a
council of his chiefs that they had not been lately
to raid their cattle, burn their villages, and carry
off their boys and girls. A Mission was sent to
Uganda begging for two teachers. The Native
Church Council met them, four men were chosen,
prayed for, and sent to Toro. Kasagama, King
of Toro, was not converted at that time; but
lately, through the indiscretion of a European
official, was unjustly imprisoned. On being re-
leased he went to Uganda and laid his case
before a commission, who censured the official

MR. A. B. FISHER ITINERATING IN TORO

and cleared the king; this was followed by his conversion, and he was baptized in Mengo. There is now a church in Toro holding 1,000 people. The first two converts in Toro were sent to the 'Mountains of the Moon' to itinerate among the people there, who had been driven from Toro by Kasagama's great-grandfather. The king's grandmother, seventy years of age, learned to read; to use her own words, 'My delight is to speak to Jesus.' So great is the spirit of giving among the people that they bring oxen, sheep, and goats, and in the case of children sweets (sugar-cane) for the collection. The speaker wished 'more at home would catch this spirit.' When we think of all this and realize that, fifteen short months ago, little children were killed and their blood dedicated to the devil, that, when a child had a pain it was burned to the bone and the smoke dedicated in like manner, that teeth were prized out with rough instruments, that it was no uncommon thing for women servants who had displeased their masters to be tied to a tree and their eyes taken out, and that, as a result of all this, there is hardly a perfectly formed man or woman in Toro, surely our hearts should be lifted up to God in thankfulness for the mighty work He has permitted His servants to do. Let

13

us pray for the king (but twenty-two years of age) that he may be kept full of the Spirit of God, and let us pray for ourselves that we may not be behindhand in Christian virtue and the love of giving to help on this good work."

In the late Indian Frontier War, the Pass of Dargai was gallantly carried by our troops. But, owing to some misunderstanding, it was almost immediately afterwards evacuated. Consequently the enemy re-occupied it, and all the hard and dangerous work had to be done over again. It had to be re-captured at the cost of many precious lives. Let not this be the case with Toro! It is now held for Christ by a small number of devoted souls. Our dear departed brother in his life and in his death claimed it for Christ. Let no negligence, or coldness, or want of self-sacrificing zeal on the part of Christians at home give the enemy of souls a chance of re-occupying it, so that the work of winning it for Christ should have to be begun all over again. Now is the time for action. All is ready. "Let us go up at once and possess the land. . . . We are well able. . . . The Lord is with us."

[Memorial Card]

In Loving and Thankful Memory of

JOHN SAMUEL CALLIS,

LATE C.M.S. MISSIONARY.

B.A. St. Catharine's Coll., Cambridge ; Wycliffe Hall, Oxford ; for three years Curate of All Saints', Woolwich ; sailed from England as one of the Uganda Party, Sept. 3rd, 1896 ; arrived at his station in Toro, Central Africa, March 13th ; called home from the field by the Lord of the harvest, April 24th, 1897.

"*Except a corn of wheat fall into the ground and die, it abideth alone ; but if it die, it bringeth forth much fruit.*" —JOHN xii. 24.

TEXT OF FAREWELL SERMON.

"The harvest truly is plenteous, but the labourers are few : pray ye therefore the Lord of the harvest, that He will send forth labourers into His harvest."—MATT. ix. 37, 38.

"He that reapeth receiveth wages, and gathereth fruit unto life eternal : that both he that soweth, and he that reapeth, may rejoice together."—JOHN iv. 36.

Deep waters crossed life's pathway,
The hedge of thorns was sharp ;
Now these lie all behind me—
Oh for a well-tuned harp ;
Oh to join Hal-le-lu-jah
With yon triumphant band,
Who sing where glory dwelleth
In Immanuel's land.

"It is true, 'Africa is waiting'; there is a real stretching out of the hands unto God."

Letter, Toro, March 15th, 1897.

LIGHT AFTER DARKNESS.

THY thoughts, O God, are deep;
  Deep as the unfathomed sea;
But they are thoughts of peace and love,
  Whate'er they seem to be.

The lightning rends the oak;
  The tempests rage and swell;
The earthquake cleaves the mighty rocks;
  The fire devours, as well.

Our fairest hopes and joys
  Wither like Jonah's gourd.
Our choicest treasures here on earth
  All vanish at Thy word.

Thou givest at Thy will,
  At Thy will tak'st away;
And those to whom our hearts most cling
  But briefly with us stay.

All this seems strange and dark,
  Wherefore? We cannnot tell.
But this we know, Thy Word says so,
  " He doeth all things well."

The cloud which is so dark,
  And turns our day to night,
When from the other side we view,
  Will shine in God's own light.

Thy glorious kingdom come,
  Thy name, Lord, hallowed be,
And Thy goodwill towards man be done
  To all eternity.

                                        J. C.

FELIXSTOWE,
  August, 1897.